Bayou Fire

Sharon E. Cathcart

Bayou Fire
by Sharon E. Cathcart
Published by CreateSpace LLC, United States of America
Copyright Sharon E. Cathcart, 2017
ISBN 978-1544887876

Photo of cover model Jason Aaron Baca by Portia Shao. Photo of Bayou St. John by Sharon E. Cathcart. Cover design by James Courtney.

Dedication

From September 2015 through November 2016, there were 21 deaths in my family or circle of friends. To say that this cumulative grief had an impact on my writing process while creating this book is to greatly understate the situation. I wish, in particular, to call out five of those who passed.

Thus, this book is dedicated to the memory of:

Angela Tracy Portis Holmes

1961-2016

A fan whom I was proud to call friend

and

David Robert Jones

1947-2016

The wild-eyed boy from Freecloud

and

Lillian Rose Porter Parker Hancock

1963-2016

A true quality friend

and

Seamus Kennedy Cathcart

2000-2016

Eras mucho gato

and

Katie Scarlett Cathcart

2001-2016

Happy Little Nobody Waggy-tail Dog

Epigraph

Thus dwelt together in love these simple Acadian farmers,—

Dwelt in the love of God and of man.

Alike were they free from

Fear, that reigns with the tyrant, and envy, the vice of republics.

Neither locks had they to their doors, nor bars to their windows;

But their dwellings were open as day and the hearts of the owners;

There the richest was poor, and the poorest lived in abundance.

— Henry Wadsworth Longfellow, *Evangeline*

Chapter One

Regardless of which direction your flight brings you
into New Orleans, there is something awe-inspiring
about that moment when the plane breaks through
the clouds. You'll either view the bayous, with their
air of mystery and solitude, or Lake Ponchartrain,
whose vastness cannot be appreciated until you see
it. The waterways of New Orleans are pure magic.
— Diana Corbett, *Time Away*

May
New Orleans

The nightmares started again, almost as soon as Diana
Corbett arrived in New Orleans. The smell of smoke ... the
flames ... the shouts of fear.

Diana hadn't had the dreams since she was five years
old and started kindergarten. Before that, starting at about
age three, she would wake up screaming that "Dolphin was
mad but Elsie will save us." During that same time, she
insisted to all and sundry that her name was not Diana, but
Banjo-lean.

Diana's parents, Andrew and Rosemary, consulted the best doctors in Seattle, including psychiatrists. They all assured the worried couple that their dark-haired daughter was fine, and that many children liked to pretend having different names.

"I wanted to be called Cinderella for a while," one kindly, grey-haired woman smiled. "She'll outgrow this Banjo-lean business."

And so it had seemed.

Diana grew up and became a well-respected travel writer, famous for her "Temporary Local" features in *Time Away* magazine. Seattle remained her home base, even though her parents moved to Spokane when her father's job transferred him. She had few friends because of all of her travels, the main one being Hope Rutherford, whom Diana had known since elementary school. Their lives were very much different, though. While Hope worked in a local insurance office, Diana would go live in a city somewhere in the world for a month and write about her experiences.

Of course, most locals didn't have their expenses paid by a glossy magazine or stay in apartments provided by vacation rental advertisers. Diana went out and saw the cities where she stayed, outside the tourist areas, but she always had a safe headquarters. Each night, she'd come home and write up her notes, upload the photos she'd taken during the day, and relate her experiences to the readers. Diana tended toward shyness, which made her an outstanding observer. She kept to herself in a corner somewhere and took in the sights and sounds ... only to leave them behind upon returning to the spartan condominium she kept in her home town.

Still, that first night in her borrowed Canal Street apartment, Diana woke up drenched in sweat, tears rolling down her face. How was it that the dream was back, almost thirty years later? She put on her bathrobe and went out to the living room to read; she knew from long experience that trying to get back to sleep after the nightmare woke her was useless.

The apartment itself was nicely furnished, with a bookcase full of novels and travel books about New Orleans and Louisiana. The overstuffed couch was ideal for napping, and there were plenty of quilts, blankets, and pillows for when the evenings turned chill. Her surroundings were comfortable, and Diana was seldom troubled by homesickness. There was no real explanation that she could think of.

Diana got herself a glass of water and pulled one of the well-thumbed novels from the shelf, reading without really paying attention to the words on the page. Eventually she felt tired enough to back to bed, but woke what felt like only a few minutes later.

A look at the clock told her it was time to get up, so she padded down the hall to the bathroom, took her various supplements and the little blue pill that regulated her dying thyroid, and got ready for her day. She had several items on her agenda, and knew that she could hit the proverbial wall at any time. Living with thyroid disease wasn't always easy, and sometimes meant rationing her energy. All the same, she met the challenge the same way she did everything else: head-on.

First things first, though: she needed to get some breakfast. She hadn't made it to the grocery store yet, but she'd seen a café that looked like it would be the perfect place to get some food and do some early-morning writing before her next appointment. Grabbing her tablet computer and sticking it into her bag, Diana stepped out of the apartment and into the humid outdoors.

"Where y'at, baby?" Miss Julie had been greeting her customers the same way for more than fifty years when they entered the Bayou Café on Decatur Street. With her white hair snugged neatly into a bun, white nylon stockings with matching Nurse-Mates shoes, and a clean handkerchief pinned to her spotless pink dress, Miss Julie was a throwback to another time.

"I'm too old to change my ways, and too young to quit working," she would say when asked why she didn't wear slacks to work. "This is how I dress for my job."

No one knew how old Miss Julie was, only that she'd been waiting tables at the Bayou Café for as long as anyone could remember. She could have been anywhere from 75 to

105 years old ... and she wasn't talking, at least not about that.

"*Chèr,* a woman who tells her age will tell you anything," she would reply, and then let forth a raucous, cackling laugh.

Every kid who grew up in the Quarter thought of Miss Julie as their auntie. Many of them came to her for advice about love, schoolwork, and parents. Miss Julie had two grown sons, Phillip and John, who lived "up North" ... which could have meant anything. She didn't talk much about them, either, other than to say that Phillip was a dentist and John an eye doctor. Nor did she talk about her late husband Allen Fredericks, other than to say he was gone, killed in a car crash over Metairie way, and good riddance. Rumor had it that he'd come home a mean drunk after the Vietnam war ended and ran off, leaving Miss Julie with two small boys.

She did talk about her sister Pauline's children, though; Miss Julie set great store by her nieces and nephews. Most of them still lived around Lafayette, where Miss Julie was born. Her favorite nephew, Amos Boudreaux, had lived up north for a while, but he was home now and had bought the Bayou Café a few years previously. He was back, Miss Julie said, after being married to a "no 'count woman" who left him for another man ... and "do you know anyone who might like to meet a nice fellow, *chère*?"

Miss Julie lived in a pleasant Garden District shotgun house, with two cats: shy orange and white Teddy, and friendly grey and white Timmy, both given to her by Amos. She rode the St. Charles and Canal streetcar lines in to work from her pink and white home, as she had every day since her husband had brought her to live in the Crescent City. The only time she'd missed was during Hurricane Katrina and its aftermath ... but as soon as the few needed repairs to her house were done, there was Miss Julie, pouring chicory-laced *café au lait* and calling her customers "baby." In other words, she was an institution in the Quarter.

The first time Miss Julie saw the young woman enter the Bayou Café, her hearty "where y'at" changed to "Welcome back, baby! Sit wherever you'd like." She was sure that she'd seen her before that Monday morning.

Diana looked at her in confusion as she took the Formica table near the window and pulled out the red-upholstered chair to sit down. "I'm sorry?"

"No *beignets* today, baby. That fool in the kitchen, Felix, had himself a little too much *fais-do-do* over at Mulate's last night, and everything coming out of the fryer is either burned to a crisp or raw in the middle. I'll be over with your hot chocolate in a minute."

"How did you know?"

Miss Julie paused and looked at Diana again.

"You know something, baby? I have no idea. I thought I knew you, but I must have confused you with someone else. Now, what can I bring you?"

"I was going to ask for beignets and cocoa."

"Oh." For the first time in a long while, Miss Julie was surprised. "Well, like I said, there won't be any beignets this morning. I'll bring you something special from the kitchen, baby. I'll be right back."

In the kitchen, Miss Julie leaned against the wall and pinched the bridge of her nose. Her head ached with the embarrassment that she felt, to say nothing of the *déjà-vu* she'd experienced.

"Tante Julie, are you all right?"

Amos had come in through the back of the café with goods from the local farmer's market and was alarmed by the look on his aunt's face. He'd tried to convince her to quit working once he'd bought the café, but she would have none of it. His brown eyes were dark with concern as he sat down the bags and pushed his thick black hair back from his forehead.

"You need to see a barber, *chèr*," his aunt smiled weakly.

"That's as may be. And you didn't answer me." He knew better than to imply that his aunt might be getting too old to continue working, or that her health was anything less than ideal. Now that he thought about it, she would probably outlive all of them. A wry smile crossed his face at the idea.

"I'm just an old fool, is all. Thought I recognized that pretty redhead in the dining room, but she's from out of town. You can tell by her voice."

Miss Julie pushed the switch on the hot chocolate machine to fill a waiting mug and cut a slice from a meaty quiche.

"This is for her. I need to sit down for a minute and collect myself, Amos. You take it out there."

"You had me at pretty redhead," he grinned, and took the food out to the dining room.

Amos had no trouble figuring out which woman to serve. She was tapping away on a tiny tablet computer in the corner, her auburn locks in a ponytail. She had the kind of soft curves that Amos had always found attractive. Her face, which showed how focused she was on her work, was more girl-next-door than fashion model; he'd always liked that, too. For a moment, Amos' heart was in his throat; like his aunt, he thought he knew the girl. But it couldn't be. Recovering quickly, he sat the food next to Diana.

"Thank you," she said, looking up at the man who now stood next to her table. His hair was a little too long, and he had a day's worth of dark beard stubble. His lips were slim, but the lines around his mouth promised a sense of humor. He had a dimple in one cheek and his eyes — so brown they were nearly black — were arresting in their intensity. He wore a pair of faded jeans, and a Tulane University t-shirt under a long-sleeved plaid flannel shirt.

"Are you the cook who had too much *fais-do-do* last night," she asked. She managed to suppress an unbidden and uncharacteristic urge to wink, but the lilt of a soft chuckle came through when she spoke.

"No such thing." A broad smile lit his handsome face. "I'm Amos, owner of the Bayou Café. My aunt took a little ill and asked me to bring this to you."

Diana took a bite of the quiche. "This is delicious; what is it?"

"My aunt's alligator cheesecake. You must be special; she usually saves it for lunch with the staff."

Diana tapped a few more keys on the computer.

"Sorry; I just wanted to make sure I mention it in my article."

"Article? Do you mind if I sit down? I'm curious."

"Please do. I'm happy to talk about it."

Amos took the chair opposite Diana, who introduced herself and explained why she was in New Orleans.

"I'm looking to give my readers a picture of the authentic New Orleans experience," she concluded.

"Now, what's authentic is going to depend on who you ask. Around here, that could mean anything from seeing every Bourbon Street dive bar to doing nothing but visiting jazz clubs on Frenchmen Street. Others will tell you that no one spends any time in the Quarter or on Frenchmen anymore and that you need to get further out. Some folks will tell you that you have to take a bunch of walking tours to really get the feel of the place, while others will tell you they hate nothing more than seeing a group of tourists traipse through their neighborhoods. There are also some parts of town that you should probably see, but not by yourself. They aren't always safe. And I'm probably talking too much," Amos finished with a laugh.

"I was going to arrange private tours ... but now that you mention it, it doesn't seem like what a local would really do. What do you recommend? I don't have a car, but I do have a Jazzy Pass."

"I could show you around," he blurted. "If you would like. I mean, the bus and the street car don't go everywhere."

Diana blushed a little. "Well ..."

"Let me at least take you to lunch; we can talk about it some more. And believe me, we Cajuns can talk you into a lot of things, so you've been warned."

"Well, all right then!. Speaking of things some of the locals don't like, though, I'm taking the St. Louis Number One cemetery tour this morning, so I need to go. Here's my card; my cell phone number is on it."

"The money from those tours goes to historical preservation; that's not quite the same as wandering around people's houses. That tour ends up at Congo Square, in Louis Armstrong Park, around noon; how about if I meet you? The place I want to show you isn't far from there."

"It's a date," Diana said, and stuck the tiny computer into her big purse. She was a little surprised at herself, agreeing to have lunch with a stranger like that. Somehow, she felt like she'd known Amos her entire life, despite never having laid eyes on the handsome Cajun before that moment.

"What do I owe," Diana asked as she stood to leave.

"My aunt would skin me alive if I charged for her gator pie. The chocolate is on the house; call it *lagniappe*. A little something extra, to welcome you to New Orleans."

Diana put a few bills on the table for a tip. "Thank you so much, Amos. I'll be looking forward to lunch."

"One more thing," Amos called after Diana. "You'll want to take a rain coat with you. It feels like we're going to be wet pretty soon."

As he watched Diana walk out the door, Amos decided that his aunt was right: he needed to see a barber.

Before lunch time.

Chapter Two

As soon as you enter a New Orleans cemetery, you know why the locals call them Cities of the Dead. The above-ground burials look like perfectly whitewashed little houses … unless they look like churches. Or, as is the case with one Hollywood star who plans to make a permanent home in St. Louis Number One, a pyramid. — Diana Corbett, *Time Away*

Back in her apartment, Diana switched to a smaller purse and pinned her hair up into a twist. She still wasn't used to seeing a redhead in the mirror; the decision to dye her hair was an impulse to which she surrendered just two days before her trip. Coming to the Crescent City as a brunette was not an option; coloring her hair had not felt so much like a choice as a compulsion. She checked herself in the mirror one last time: green blouse, with flat shoes nearly the same shade, accompanied by jeans that showed off her curves. As she took Amos' advice to don a rain coat, she decided that she'd do.

In fact, she was having trouble keeping her mind on anything but Amos Boudreaux and their lunch date. Although it made no sense, Diana couldn't shake the feeling that she'd met him before.

"I'm imagining things," she told herself as she headed out the door for her tour.

The tour itself was a non-stop view of New Orleans history through the eyes of its departed. Starting at Our Lady of Guadalupe on North Rampart Street, once called the Mortuary Church because it was attached to the cemetery, the guide talked about the various yellow fever plagues and how they had affected the city. Once inside the gates of St. Louis No. 1, Diana and her fellow travelers learned about Homer Plessy of Plessy v. Ferguson fame, chess savant Paul Morphy, whose Royal Street mansion was now a popular restaurant, voodoo queen Marie Laveau, and Delphine LaLaurie, whose house at the corner of Royal and Governor Nicholls was reputed to be the most haunted mansion in New Orleans.

From the cemetery, the group moved to Louis Armstrong Park, with its bronze statues of notables like its namesake jazz legend and Big Chief Tootie Montana. It was there that they discussed Congo Square and the Sunday activities of both slaves and free people of color that took place at the site.

Diana could hardly wait to share the story with her readers.

At the very end of the tour, there were card readers and palmists aplenty waiting to take a few dollars in exchange for their services. Diana couldn't resist; she sat down in front of a palmist who looked at both of her hands, front and back. The older woman looked her deep in the eyes for a moment, and then studied her hands again.

"You come from far away, and you have been many places."

Diana didn't think that was much of a stretch, to be honest, but she nodded. That was when things became personal.

"You have an illness that you conceal from others; you must know when to trust. One who loves you will not care. You've been here before, and you've come through much to return — even through smoke and fire. There is a dark man who watches over you; he, too, has gone through much to return to you. Your hearts have been together many times."

The part about her illness shook Diana a little bit, but the rest sounded like hokum ... until she thought about Amos' deep brown eyes. Surely it was a coincidence.

She thanked the reader, paid the modest charge to which she'd agreed, and made her way out of the park. She couldn't help noticing the homeless contingent there; that was something every city she'd lived in or visited had in common. That it seemed to be a universal problem did not make it any less heartbreaking for Diana.

Amos gave himself one last look in the bedroom mirror of his St. Ann Street cottage before heading out to meet Diana. The barber at his favorite Magazine Street shop had done just what he asked ... but now he wasn't sure why he'd wanted it to begin with. He hadn't worn his unruly black hair this short since he was a little boy. Back then, he'd slicked it back with water; now it was held in place with pomade. The straight-razor shave, followed by a shot of Irish whisky, hadn't hurt matters when it came to his appearance — and his courage.

It had been a long time since he'd done so many impulsive things in one morning.

Without really thinking, he reached into a drawer and pulled out a small gold hoop that he slipped into his left earlobe. He hadn't worn an earring since his college days, but he liked the way it looked with his new haircut.

He stopped by the café to check on his aunt one last time on his way to Congo Square.

"Lord 'a' mercy, Amos!" Miss Julie took in his white shirt, tight jeans, polished boots, and new haircut. "You remind me of when you were a little boy. Remember how you used to pretend you were a fireman?"

That wasn't entirely true, though, Amos thought. From the ages of five to about seven, he occasionally dressed up in a fresh white shirt and talked about going to New Orleans to save the people from the fire. He also wanted to be called by his middle name, insisting that he wasn't Amos. He wasn't pretending to be a fireman at all; in fact, he was acting out a recurring dream. Still, everyone assumed that he would be a firefighter when he grew up, and they were surprised when he went "up North" and became a lawyer.

"You're awfully duded up for lunch, though. I think you like that girl from this morning," Miss Julie teased her nephew.

"You told me I needed a haircut," he replied. "I thought I should get one before I take Diana to meet Miss Leah."

"Diana," Miss Julie smiled. "So you got her name."

"You saw us chatting, Tante Julie," he teased back. "I'm just taking her to Miss Leah's to help with her article."

"Of course you are, *chèr*."

"Do you need me to help close?"

"Boy, I was closing this restaurant when you and my own sons were still little. I can do this without your help. Just be sure you're back in time to help set up for breakfast tomorrow!"

Amos was leaning on a sleek black car outside of Louis Armstrong Park when Diana finished her tour and reading. She couldn't help appreciating his good looks as she walked over to meet him. He wore a classic tan raincoat over his shirt and jeans, and managed to look both casual and dressy at the same time.

"I've never seen a car like this," she said by way of greeting. "What is it?" She mentally compared its low-slung, sporty lines to her sensible Toyota sedan back in

Seattle. Her own car came up wanting by quite a long chalk.

"It's a Detomaso Pantera; this black beauty was my gift to myself after I passed the bar exam. My oldest brother gave me a Matchbox Pantera when I was a little kid, and I always told people I'd have a real one someday. And I'm here to tell you that it is about the most temperamental machine I've ever come across. I'm always fixing some damn thing in that engine. Hop in," he said, holding the passenger door open for her. "We'll get down someplace special for lunch. I want you to meet Miss Leah."

"Get down? As in dancing?"

Amos had a rich laugh that she didn't expect, despite the musicality of his accent. "No, *chèr*! It means we're stopping there. I can see I'm going to have to educate you. Ordinarily we'd walk, but I don't want you getting soaked once this rain gets going."

The restaurant into which Amos led Diana turned out to be a white tablecloth establishment disguised by a plain brick exterior. A tiny Black woman greeted them as they came in.

"Amos Boudreaux! Where y'at, baby? How's your mama and them?"

"I'm good, Miss Leah. Miss Leah, this is Diana Corbett. She's a writer for *Time Away* magazine, and she's in town doing an article. Diana, this is Miss Leah. She's been cooking here since before I was born. The place is named after her husband."

"You'd better believe it," the old woman laughed. "And I'm still the best cook in town. Baby, you two have a seat and I'll have them bring you out some of my fried chicken. No buffet for you two; this is special. I got to get back to my kitchen. Now, Amos, you tell your auntie and your mama I said hello."

She kissed him on the cheek and was gone as fast as she and her walker could go.

The food was just as good as Miss Leah promised. Amos kept a running commentary going as they ate, telling Diana about how civil rights leaders used to meet at "the restaurant" to discuss strategy.

"That's what they called this place: the restaurant. At the time, it was the only one where Black people could come in to have a sit-down meal in New Orleans."

This history, he maintained, was just as important as the food. He also talked about the art on the walls; the restaurant housed one of the finest collections of African-American art in the country.

Diana hoped she wasn't staring at Amos; she couldn't remember the last time she'd seen a man that good-looking. He'd been to the barber since she saw him at breakfast, and the slicked-back hair he now sported showed off the planes of his face. The sleeves of his white shirt were rolled up to show nicely-muscled forearms, and tight dark-wash jeans hugged his slim hips. She even liked the rakish air his small gold earring gave him. It was nice to have an escort who seemed to know everyone; that he was handsome as all get-out didn't hurt.

Then she chided herself for those shallow thoughts; looks were not everything, after all. She'd learned that the hard way. Handsome is as handsome does; her grandma had said that all the time, and she'd been right. It had only taken one good-looking man with a shallow heart to make Diana wary.

After lunch, Amos drove them to a small white building on Henriette deLille Street that he told her had once been a funeral parlor. Inside, he said, was some of the most important information that Leah could put in her story.

"This neighborhood, the Tremé, is the first real African-American neighborhood in America. Inside here is the Backstreet Cultural Museum. Sylvester Francis, the man who started it, wanted to preserve the culture of the New Orleans Black Indians, including their amazing parade costumes.

"The Black Indians came about because slaves would escape and go hide with the Choctaw and Biloxi. They'd marry and have children, of course. They first had a Carnival parade in the 1890s, and this little building is where the most information about the culture lives."

The museum was only two rooms, but it was crammed with costumes, memorabilia, and historical information. Only four pictures in each room were permitted, and Diana had a hard time deciding where to start. There was so much information, let alone the clothing. The heavily beaded costumes must have weighed in excess of a hundred pounds.

"The uptown *krewes* made these three dimensional suits," Amos explained as he indicated an elaborate lavender suit with a castle extending out from the chest, "and the downtown *krewes* made the flat mosaics. You could tell what area a *krewe* came from by how their suits were designed. It used to be that they'd burn these suits on Ash Wednesday and start a new one for next Carnival and Mardi Gras, but the information was kind of dying out. That statue of Big Chief Tootie Montana in Armstrong Park is a huge deal to the *krewes*."

Amos walked Diana back to the car and she gave him the address for her apartment. The rain had begun in earnest by then.

Amos dropped Diana off in front her apartment building after exacting a promise to meet him at Mulate's restaurant for dinner. "It's the best place for Cajun dancing on a Monday, and I promise there's no such thing as too much *fais-do-do*," he'd said, and she'd agreed. It seemed like a great idea. Diana thanked him for a lovely afternoon, pulled up the hood of her own tan raincoat, and bolted for entry of her apartment building. She gave Amos a wave as she unlocked the front door and went inside.

Diana typed up her notes from the day; she hadn't expected to learn so much. A nap would do her good before dinner, though; so she slipped in between the sheets.

Almost immediately, the dream began. She was beating on a locked door and crying out for help. She woke herself up and realized, for the first time since childhood, that she hadn't been calling for anyone name Elsie at all.

The name on her lips was Alcide.

She looked at the clock and realized she had only a little time to freshen up. Her hair hung loose to just past her shoulder blades; she ran a comb through it and fixed her makeup. A fresh top, this time a yellow t-shirt, and tennis shoes completed her outfit. Amos had told her the place was casual and that she should just wear something comfortable.

Chapter Three

When you think of New Orleans, it's inevitable that you think of both good music and good food. — Diana Corbett, *Time Away*

Amos was already waiting at a table when she got to the restaurant, which was across the street from the Riverwalk. He'd washed the pomade from his black hair, and switched to a blue chambray shirt.

It seemed like everyone in town knew him, because people kept stopping by their table to say hello. After a while, Amos confessed that he'd been a regular here when he went to Tulane University, teaching Cajun dances to newcomers and enjoying the opportunity to dance with experienced partners as well.

"I still come in from time to time," he finished. "Do you want to give it a whirl?"

"I suspect I should watch for a while before I even try," Diana said.

"Let's worry about dinner first, then. The food here is good, but the music is always first-rate. And I know a guy who's a pretty good teacher when it comes to the dancing part." He winked at her, and she noticed how long and thick his lashes were.

Diana wasn't accustomed to attention from men this handsome, and she couldn't help wondering whether he was flirting with her or not. She decided to just relax and enjoy herself.

Amos was asked to dance by one of the regulars, and soon he was out on the floor moving to a lively swing tune. Diana couldn't help admiring how smoothly he led his partner through the steps. When he came back to the table and asked her to join him for the next song, she gave an enthusiastic "yes."

The two-step wasn't as hard as she'd thought it might be, and Amos was easy to dance with.

"It feels like we've done this a million times," she said. "You're a good teacher."

"Mmm hmm," he replied. Amos wasn't thinking so much about the steps as he was about how good it felt to hold Diana in his arms, even if it was just for dancing.

The next number was more bluesy, and Amos drew a little Diana closer to him. The sensual rhythm of the music soon lent itself to their movements; their dancing itself was like a lover's caress. Diana didn't want it to end; she couldn't remember the last time she'd been so attracted to a man.

After the song, Amos held Diana's hand as they returned to their table to wait for their dinner. Both were quiet … and keenly aware of how natural it felt to stay connected that way.

Amos recommended the crawfish "triple play," which turned out to be just as good he'd promised. Crawfish *etouffée,* crawfish *au gratin,* and fried crawfish tails gave Diana a chance to taste the local favorite while still getting some variety. It was rich and delicious, and Diana was glad that she'd be doing a lot of walking; there was no denying the caloric content of the wonderful food, and she'd need to be careful.

"Would you call this authentic, then?" Diana asked after the dishes were cleared away.

"I would call it as authentic as you'll find in New Orleans. This city is more Creole than Cajun. If you're interested, I can make some phone calls and see about getting you out to Cajun country."

"I'd love it, Amos. Truly."

"Then consider it done."

Neither Amos nor Diana wanted the evening to end; they danced together for a few more hours and Amos drove Diana back to her apartment.

Neither slept well that night, for thinking of the other

When sleep eluded Amos, he got up and switched on his computer. The *Time Away* website gave him an opportunity to read a few of Diana's articles. There were stories about her living in Paris, Boston, San Francisco …

all over the world, really. Her articles not only showed everyday experiences like grocery shopping or taking the subway, but also attending the opera and art exhibits. One moment she was helping in a soup kitchen, the next she was at the symphony. Yet another photo showed that she was in a crowd of protestors, right in the middle so she could capture the action around her. It looked like such a glamorous existence to Amos; Diana Corbett had been all over the world. The comments on the articles showed that her fan base was far from small, too. More than one person wrote about how much they enjoyed traveling along with her from their homes and learning so much about new people and places.

Amos returned to bed and finally fell asleep, thinking about how very impressed he was with the woman whom he'd just met ... and wondering anew why it felt as though he'd known her before.

Chapter Four

Don't be surprised by the friendliness in the Crescent City. The locals, or Yats, will welcome you like a long-lost relative. — Diana Corbett, *Time Away*

The following morning, Amos phoned his mother and asked whether he could bring a travel writer friend out to visit.

"I want her to see where we all live, Mommy. And please, don't make a fuss. This is just a quiet visit to the Cajun country for her article."

"Of course I won't make a fuss, Amos. Just a nice family dinner."

"Thank you, Mommy. I look forward to bringing Diana out to meet you."

As soon as she was off the phone with her son, Pauline Boudreaux made calls to family members in Eunice, Opelousas, Mamou, and even smaller towns.

"Amos is bringing a lady friend out to visit," she explained. "Just bring something for the gumbo pot. We want to show her a nice time. No fuss, though, you hear?"

Of course, "lady friend" was interpreted by brothers, sisters and cousins alike as "girlfriend," and they were eager to meet the woman Amos was bringing home. Naturally, the "fussing" commenced almost immediately.

During the week, Diana busied herself with visits to museums, parks, and restaurants. She checked out the newest celebrity chef establishments in the Central Business District on the same day she visited the oldest lunch counters in the Bywater. Museums large and small gave her a picture of life and culture throughout the Crescent City's long and colorful history. It seemed there was always something just around the corner that she was sure her readers would love. There were even hidden gems, like the labyrinth in Audubon Park, that she wanted to highlight.

Amos phoned her each evening to see how her day had gone ... or so he told himself. The truth was that he enjoyed hearing both her voice and her enthusiasm for a city that he loved. What he didn't admit to himself was that chatting with her made his little house seem a lot less empty. Despite its cheerful yellow paint and green storm shutters — to say nothing of his elderly landlady Mrs. Delacourt, in the cottage right next door, who was always ready to share a cup of coffee and whatever gossip she heard from her daughters — the place sometimes felt cold and lonely. Diana didn't just chatter small talk, though; she was thoughtful in her discussions about the places she'd visited that day. Her insights into his own city sometimes surprised Amos; it was a long time since he'd seen New Orleans through the eyes of a newcomer.

When Diana told him she had plans to visit Preservation Hall for a late show one evening, Amos insisted on meeting her there. He walked over from his house and joined her in the line that snaked down St. Peter Street. Once inside, they sat on the floor cushions in the very front, listening to traditional jazz played by some of the finest musicians Diana had ever heard. When she whispered that her back was bothering her a little, Amos moved closer so that she could lean against him. He put an arm around her waist and she settled in with a sigh. She was close enough now that Amos could smell her perfume, which was subtle but intoxicating. He recognized it as a signature scent from a French Quarter perfumer on Chartres Street; it was perfect for her. And it made him realize how much he wanted to make love to the woman whose head rested on his shoulder.

After the show, they stopped in at a restaurant just down St. Peter from the Hall to get something to eat. Diana tried *callas* for the first time; the rice fritters had a hint of cinnamon and nutmeg. She declared them delicious, and scribbled down a few notes about the dish to share with her readers. Amos told her about how the Black women used to sell them on the streets, carrying heavy baskets filled with the delicious treats by balancing them on their heads.

"You could buy just about anything on the streets at one point. Someone might be selling jambalaya straight from the pot, or pieces of sugar cane. That's where the French Market really got started, with the street vendors. The history of this city's food alone is amazing," he said.

"You really are a font of knowledge," Diana replied.

"I love this city. It's like no other place I've ever been. It calls to you when you're not here, telling you to come home."

As they walked down Royal Street back to Canal together, Amos told Diana that he'd arranged for her to visit his family in Lafayette that weekend and asked her to come to the restaurant Saturday afternoon. "Bring a bag; you're invited to spend Saturday night and see what a family *fais-do-do* looks like."

He also invited her to join him two weeks hence at a black-tie event for Tulane alumni, which would be held in the New Orleans Museum of Art at City Park. She said yes, and then wondered what on earth she was going to wear. She hadn't expected to attend a formal event on this particular trip. At least she had time to look for a dress.

Chapter Five

Do your best to get outside the city limits; there's a lot of interesting history in Louisiana, and many things to see and do. — Diana Corbett, *Time Away*

Diana came to the café on Saturday afternoon in a taxi; walking through the Quarter with an overnight bag felt like a recipe for exhaustion before the journey ever began. She was surprised to see the line by the back door. Amos, Miss Julie, and Felix, the cook, were handing out sack lunches and paper cups of iced tea. Diana pitched in to help, not even waiting to be asked. After the last bag was handed out, Amos explained.

"There are still people here in New Orleans who lost everything during Hurricane Katrina. Some folks never made their way back here after evacuating, but many who did manage to get home came back to nothing. There were another couple of bad floods since then. One of these times I'll take you driving through the lower Ninth Ward. There are places where there's still no electricity or phone, and where whole blocks that used to have houses are empty. Since we only open for breakfast and lunch, I decided that we'd hand out food to those in need on Saturday afternoons. No questions asked. Someone from the homeless shelter picks things up after we close during the week, too. Food shouldn't go to waste when people are hungry.

"I need to pack a bag; my place is up on St. Ann. Let's go." He grabbed the handle of Diana's little wheelie bag. "We're close enough to walk."

"Are you sure you won't join us, Miss Julie," Diana asked.

"I have things to do on Sunday, like makin' groceries and goin' to church. My sister and them will keep you entertained without my help." The older woman looked out the window. "No. You all go on."

Miss Julie had other reasons for not wanting to visit her former home town, but now was hardly the time to share them.

Amos' house was furnished in masculine style, with brown leather couches and a large flat-screen television in the living room. He offered Diana something to drink while he packed, and she accepted a glass of lemonade.

In its own way, Diana realized, Amos' home was just as barren as her own. Diana didn't have pets or plants, because she traveled so much for her job, and the furniture was utilitarian at best. At least Amos' couch was comfortable. She noticed a toy car on his desk; it was a miniature version of his Pantera. This was obviously the car he'd played with as a child. A beautiful acoustic guitar stood on a stand close by a two-person dining table in the little kitchen. It would be easier to play sitting on one of the dining-chairs than the leather couch, Diana thought.

For his part, Amos was in the master bedroom throwing things into an overnight bag without too much thought. When he put his shaving kit into the bag, he grabbed a couple of condoms from the box in the nightstand. It couldn't hurt to be prepared, just in case. If he didn't need them, that was fine too. It was all up to Diana.

"Can I ask you something," Diana said when he came back down with his bag.

"Sure. What is it?"

"You said there were whole neighborhoods in the lower Ninth Ward where nothing had been fixed since Hurricane Katrina. Why not?"

Amos sat down next to her on the couch.

"Well, that's kind of a complicated story. To sum it all up, the folks in government at that time sat down with the construction companies and a map and told them to focus on recovering certain parts of town. And those parts of town, *chère*? They weren't where the poor Black folks lived. They focused on fixing the rich parts of town. It's a damn shame, but it's the truth."

Diana sat silently for a moment.

"I don't know what to say," she finally ventured. "I would think they'd want to help everyone in this town."

"Not everyone here on Earth is as good as they might be, *chère*. That's the only explanation I have." He stood up and extended a hand to her. "Let's get going."

During the drive to Lafayette, Amos found himself chattering a lot more than usual once they were out of range of his favorite radio station, WWOZ. He started out by talking about the history of the region, and about the Acadian *dérangement* that drove his ancestors out of Nova Scotia. Soon, talk turned more personal.

"I had a decent life in Chicago as a lawyer, I won't deny it. But then I had a chance to come back home and work for a non-profit dedicated to preserving the Louisiana French language, which some people call Cajun French. It's very much endangered at this point, with less than half the speakers that we had twenty years ago. There's a long-standing movement to preserve our music, and the same to preserve our food. But the language preservation project is new. There's kind of an Acadian pride thing that's been going on since a little bit before I was born, but it's still not common.

"I worked full-time for the Bayou Cultural Society for a while. Then the chance came up to buy the café where my aunt works, so I took it. I still work part-time for the Society.

"My wife didn't like the idea of me leaving a partnership in Chicago to come back down here. We divorced a long while ago. She's a nurse up there somewhere."

He glanced over at Diana before returning his attention to the road.

"Sorry. I didn't mean to go on like that."

"No, it's all right. This is great information for my article."

As soon as the words came out of her mouth, she regretted them. She didn't want Amos to think she was using him to further her project.

"About the language preservation, I mean. I think people who read the story would want to know that," she explained.

"We're also working on preserving Kouri-Vini, which is Louisiana Creole. There are fewer than a thousand speakers left. You'll want to mention that in your article, too. We can't let these aspects of our culture die, and the more people who know about them, the better. Seems like, outside of this state, people don't care all that much. Hell, even inside this state it seems that people don't care all that much."

Diana was grateful when talk turned to family. Learning that Amos was the youngest of eleven children floored her.

"French Catholics, duty-bound to make a mess of babies for the church and the Lord." He laughed. "I'd be happy with one or two myself, but that would be it. I saw how hard my mother's life was. My dad worked out on the oil rigs, so we were okay financially. Not rich, but okay.

Still, it's hard on a woman having so many children to care for, and my daddy was gone for weeks and months at a time out on the Gulf. Harmon, my oldest brother, was eighteen when I came along. That's a long time between oldest and youngest. All of my siblings have kids except Harm and me. He lost his wife to breast cancer some while back and never re-married.

"I can't imagine how much harder it would have been for all of us if my dad had been a shrimper or a fisherman. That's a chancy way to make a living nowadays, and it wasn't that much easier when I was a kid. There are older folks who've been on the bayou their entire lives, living that subsistence lifestyle. Some of them came up speaking French rather than English, and they sound a lot different from me when they talk. Still, the thing about bayou folk is that they'd give you the hat off their heads on a hot day. You couldn't ask for a more generous bunch. There's always space at the table for one more."

Diana was an only child; it was hard to imagine growing up in such a crowded household, let alone the money worries that had to come with it. Somehow, though, Amos made it sound like fun as he talked about how each child was expected not only to do his or her share around the house but to play an instrument and learn to dance in order to keep their dying culture alive.

"I think the preservation thing is in my blood," he continued. "And my ex-wife hated that. When I took the job with the Bayou Cultural Society, she told me she had no intention of coming back to Louisiana and being married to a swamp rat. Those were her words. I had no idea how much she hated this place when we met at Tulane. But she couldn't wait to get out."

"I can't imagine that feeling, to be honest. I've always loved Seattle, and have never really thought about living anywhere else on a permanent basis."

"Well, Kelly grew up in the Irish Channel, which was not the nicest part of town back then. I guess she felt embarrassed about her people. She wanted to go live somewhere that no one would knew where she came from. She never said a thing about it until I wanted to come back, and then I got a real earful." His expression was rueful. "Truth is, none of my folks much cared for her. They tried to tell me, but I can be a stubborn son of a bitch, and I wouldn't listen to anyone. She was the prettiest girl I'd ever seen, and she loved me. That was all I cared about at the time."

Chapter Six

Sharing food and traditions keeps them alive for future generations. — Diana Corbett, *Time Away*

"Grandmama, Uncle Amos and his toot-toot are here!" The dark-haired little boy who answered the door hollered toward the back of the house as he let them in.

"Jimmy!" Amos picked him up around the waist and swung him into the air. "Pretty soon you'll be too big for me to do this!"

Once back on the floor, Jimmy looked Diana up and down. "Your toot-toot sure is pretty, Uncle Amos."

"What's a toot-toot?" Diana asked, puzzled.

"It means sweetheart. Comes from the French. And Jimmy here is definitely talking out of turn." Amos actually turned a little red. "Mommy! This is Diana Corbett, the writer I told you about." He seemed relieved to change the subject.

Amos' mother, Pauline, was so tiny that it seemed impossible that she'd had ten children before him. Like her sister, Miss Julie, it was impossible to tell her age. Pauline's white hair was cut short, and she wore comfortable-looking slacks and sneakers on her feet. She wrapped her arms around Diana like she was a long-lost friend.

"*Chère*, I'm so glad my boy brought you out. I've got gumbo on the stove, and we'll have music and dancing on the deck until the mosquitos chase us inside. Amos, you're going to play."

It was not a question.

There were so many brothers, sisters, cousins and in-laws that Diana was sure she'd never remember anyone's name but Jimmy's. He attached himself to her immediately, chattering a mile a minute.

"Reckon my daddy owes Uncle Harm a nickel," he was saying. "Uncle Harm said he'd bet a nickel that Uncle Amos was bringing a red-haired girl to visit. Uncle Harm … that's Harmon … is the oldest and Uncle Amos is the youngest. When I grow up, I'm gonna have a red-haired toot-toot like you."

"Jimmy Arceneaux, you stop plaguing Miss Diana. Go play with your cousins," one of the women said. Her dark hair was cut in a practical, chin-length bob and she wore jeans and a sweatshirt.

Turning to Diana, she continued. "Annie Arceneaux. I'm Amos' sister. I figured I'd better reintroduce myself … and get my son out of your hair. In case you hadn't guessed, he purely idolizes my baby brother, and wants to be just like him when he grows up. Don't let him plague you too much, or you'll never have a moment's peace."

Diana laughed. "He was no bother, really. And I guess it was your husband who's lost the nickel."

"Indeed. Billy couldn't believe it when you came in. Amos has always been partial to redheads. Heck, just about every girl he dated wound up dyeing her hair if he asked how she thought she'd look as a redhead. That no-account Kelly he married was an Irish redhead. Left him for another man when she and Amos lived in Chicago.

"And now, look at me running on just the way my boy did. I'd better go help Mommy lay the table."

Diana soon felt justifiably overwhelmed and made her way to a quiet corner. It was there Amos found her, cross-legged on the floor, petting the ears of an elderly hound dog.

"I see you found Belle," he said, lowering himself to sit next to her. "You can count on her to find a quiet spot when the kids get to be too much. I got her for Mommy when Daddy died; she was just a pup. Now she's almost ten years old."

"I do the same thing at parties. In fact, half the time you'll find me in the other room with somebody's dog or cat," Diana replied. "I hear that your brother-in-law had to pay up a bet because you brought a redhead to visit."

"Cajuns will bet on any damn thing," he laughed. "I've always liked redheads, it's true. But the girl under that hair is what matters most. I should know; I married the meanest redhead ever born."

"Your nephew also tells me that he plans to have a red-haired toot-toot like me when he grows up." She smiled.

"Am I going to lose you to a six-year-old?" Amos grinned at her.

"You never can tell; he's pretty charming. I suspect it runs in the family."

Flirting with Amos was an awful lot of fun, Diana thought. She felt relaxed and safe with him and his family.

"Which one is Harmon, again?"

Amos indicated a tall man whose black hair was greying at the temples. The resemblance between the two men was so strong that Diana felt like she was seeing Amos' future.

"You look very much alike," she remarked.

"Sure enough, but he's got those grey-green Cajun eyes that seem to slay the ladies. It surely would be nice if he'd meet someone, but he doesn't seem to be looking too hard."

Jimmy came running up to the two.

"Grandmama says to tell you that supper is on out back and to bring you to the table," he pronounced.

Amos helped Diana up from the floor, giving her hand a squeeze as they went outside.

Supper was served around picnic tables out on the deck. Diana sat between Jimmy and Amos, with the former continuing to chatter whenever he wasn't chewing.

There was gumbo, boudin sausage from the store in Mowata ("It's my favorite," Pauline confided as she passed

45

the serving platter), and barbecue bread ("Bunny bread is the best kind," Jimmy informed her solemnly) to pull straight off the loaf and mop up sauce from the bottom of the bowl. Ice buckets full of beer and soda pop were out as well. Everyone was laughing, chatting, and enjoying the food.

"What do you think of the dinner, Miss Diana?" Jimmy asked during a quiet moment.

"Everything tastes so good," she replied. "And I can't remember when I had more fun at supper. I'm lucky to have such nice hosts. Usually when I'm working on a story, I eat at restaurants or in my apartment. I am glad that Amos asked me out here to meet all of you. This has been wonderful."

"You're the Diana Corbett who writes those travel articles, aren't you?" Annie asked. "I surely do admire *Time Away*, and I look forward to your stories. Why, you just bring us right into all of those places with you."

Diana blushed. "That's very kind of you."

"What kind of places have you been?" Billy asked.

"Well, I was lucky enough to spend a month in Paris; that was great. And I really enjoyed my time in London, Boston, and San Francisco. There were some other places I didn't like as much, but I still had to try to put a brave face on it for the readers. It can be hard to live somewhere that you don't feel like you fit in at all."

"Sure sounds like me in Chicago," Amos said quietly. "But the good news is that I was able to come home where I belong." He slipped his hand into Diana's under the table.

After supper, the instruments came out. It seemed that just about everybody played something. After just a few chords of a song, Amos took Diana out to join him in a waltz.

"I loved this song when I was a boy," he said. "Mommy had an old record of it by Rose Maddox, and I played that thing to death."

They danced as though they'd waltzed together a thousand times before, as Harmon played violin, and their mother played the mandolin and sang about a tramp on the street.

Amos brought Diana closer to him, still moving in time to the music, and kissed her forehead.

"Thank you for coming out here with me." The second kiss dropped gently on her lips.

"Amos Boudreaux, you stop kissing on that girl and go get your squeeze box," Pauline called after the song ended. "I've a mind to hear '*Jolie Blon*'."

Turning to Diana, she said "You sit down here with me, *chère*, and get ready for a treat. My boy Amos can sing!"

Amos went into the house and came out with an old Sterling button accordion. When he sat down in the gathering dusk and started to play, Diana couldn't take her eyes off of him. He was quite the package, with his dark good looks and talent. Harmon joined in with his violin, and the two men harmonized beautifully. Amos' baritone joined in with Harm's tenor seamlessly.

"You should have seen us in the old days," Pauline was saying. "Those Kershaw and Savoy boys would come around and we'd have a real *laissez les bon temps rouler*."

She stopped and watched Diana watching Amos.

"You look like you're fallin' in love with my boy, *chère*. I think you must be, me. You can't stop watching him."

"I don't know, Miss Pauline. Maybe. It feels like I've known him forever. I know I like him, and if nothing else I've found a new friend." The words sounded weak, even to Diana. Still, it was the truth. It was just too soon to call it love.

"Hmm. Reminds me of my sister Julie, with that Antoine Robicheaux. He still lives just up the road, him. He was her sweetheart until that no-account soldier boy Allen Fredericks turned her head with promises of living all over the world. She married that damn fool, and the furthest he ever took her was to New Orleans. Antoine never married, and Julie won't come out here anymore out of pride.

"Don't you make the mistake my sister did, *chère*. That boy of mine is a good man, him. And if your heart is tellin' you that you love him, you should listen to it.

"Now, look at me goin' on. I'm missin' my song."

Diana still didn't think it was possible to really be in love with someone on such short acquaintance. They barely knew each other. Still, she felt some stirring that was more than just the tickle of infatuation, and there was no denying how comfortable she felt with Amos and his family.

Diana went back inside for a few minutes to scribble some notes about the food and music. When she walked by the fireplace, she noticed a number of photos on the mantel and went to investigate them. One of them was a much younger Amos, in a rather peculiar tassel-covered shirt and matching pointed hat, riding a black horse. A strand of large wooden beads circled his neck, draping down his chest.

"That's Cajun Mardi Gras," Annie said, coming up behind her. "It's not like what they do over in New Orleans. Out here, all the men dress in traditional costumes and ride horses from house to house, trying to get the women to give up something for the gumbo pot. At the end, everyone puts the ingredients together and there's a big batch of soup to share. Amos was always one of the best riders, with those long legs of his. That black mare belonged to a neighbor, and they'd always let Amos borrow her for Mardi Gras. Every year he managed to get some woman to give up the chicken; we said he just batted his eyelashes and that was all she wrote. The chicken was the big prize for the stew pot."

"That's fascinating," Diana said. "Thank you!" It seemed that Amos was even more multi-talented than she'd thought.

She followed Annie back outside. There, Amos, Harmon, and Billy were singing an a cappella song in

French. Diana was able to understand only about half of it, something about the keys to the prison, but it didn't matter. The three of them sounded marvelous together.

Later that evening, Amos and a slew of other men stood off to one side of the deck, smoking thin black cigars and drinking Abita beer straight from the bottle. Diana stood off to the other side, looking out over the railing and thinking, while the men talked and laughed. They gabbed away in a dialect of French that bore little relation to what she'd briefly studied in school and she could only catch a few words here and there. She understood why Amos felt so protective of his culture; it was more than just food and language. It was part of his identity.

Her offer to help tidy up was refused by Pauline. "We can save the dishes without bothering our guest."

Annie'd explained that it meant washing and putting everything away.

How was she going to fit all of this into her article? Her editor was going to think she'd lost her mind.

And did she even want to put it all in her story? Maybe Pauline was right about her falling in love. Or maybe she needed to write a different kind of article entirely: one that showed the sense of pride that she'd seen everywhere she went in Louisiana. She hadn't seen anything like it since her sojourn in Paris.

Amos broke away from the group and came over to join her. "You all right, Diana?"

"I'm fine." She turned to face him. "What language were you fellows speaking just now?"

"Kouri-Vini … Louisiana Creole. Not too many people speak it anymore, so we like to practice. Besides, it comes in handy when we don't want the kids to know what we bought for their birthdays. Thanks for asking. Would you like to learn a phrase or two?"

"Sure; I'm game."

"Okay. Let's do something easy. I live in Lafayette is '*mo rès a Lafayette.*' The syntax and pronouns are different from French, but some things are the same."

"So, I would say *mo rès a Seattle*, to tell someone where I'm from."

"Well, the phrase for I'm from Lafayette is '*mo sor a Lafayette*,' so it's a little different." Amos paused for a moment; when he resumed, his voice was quiet. "You surely do look pretty in the moonlight, Diana."

"And in Kouri-Vini?"

He could tell she was teasing, but he looked deep into her eyes and whispered "*To bèl*" as he caressed her cheek. It was "you're beautiful," not "you're pretty," but he wasn't in the mood for quibbling over niceties.

He was prevented from saying more by the arrival of young Jimmy Arceneaux, holding an empty jar. "Miss Diana, come with me and I'll show you how to catch fireflies. I promise we don't keep 'em; we let 'em go. But I reckon you should know how so you can talk about it in your story. You can come too, Uncle Amos."

"Well, I guess I'd better! I don't want you running away with my red-headed toot-toot! I need to watch out."

Jimmy carefully trapped fireflies in the old Blue Plate mayonnaise jar and showed them to Diana. "You have to be quick. But you can do it. We have to let 'em go, though. Uncle Harm, he says they're endangered. That means that they might not be around forever. So we need to respect them and leave them out in nature. You try, Miss Diana."

After several failures, Diana captured one of the insects in the jar and watched it glow for a moment before releasing it.

It was getting darker and they all went back to the house together, Jimmy chattering a mile a minute. "Maybe my uncle Amos will take you out to our fishin' camp. Do you know about that? It's where we go fishin' when the weather's good, and it's only a little ways from here. You have to be careful about logs out there. Some of them ain't logs, they're alligators. And you need to watch out for them. We don't have alligators too much here in Lafayette, though. That's more out in the bayous and such."

Chapter Seven

There are good reasons why songs are written about the Louisiana moonlight. — Diana Corbett, *Time Away*

Amos put his arm around Diana's shoulders and they lagged a little bit behind. "I'm so glad you came out here. On the way home tomorrow, I'll stop by that fishing camp Jimmy was rattling on about; it really is beautiful."

"It was kind of you to invite me." She felt suddenly shy; she'd only met Amos a week ago and, despite her feelings of *déjà vu*, that was a very short time indeed for her to feel what was welling up in her heart.

He stopped and pulled her closer, then covered her mouth with his, gently at first and then deeply. She returned his kiss, feeling a heat in her body that had been dormant for too long. The sweet taste of cheroot was surprisingly sensual on his tongue.

Amos was the one to break away. "My god, *chère*. I …"

She stroked her thumb across his lips, removing the bit of her lipstick that remained.

"Not another word, Amos Boudreaux," she said quietly. "I wanted it just as much as you did. In fact, I would very much like for you to kiss me again."

Amos took her at her word, and the two of them stayed in the embrace for a few minutes.

"We'd best get inside before they send out a search party," Amos said at last. He took Diana's hand and the two walked the rest of the way to the house.

"Miss Diana, you and Uncle Amos need to hurry up and put on your pajamas," Jimmy exclaimed as she and Amos came back inside "Uncle Harm's gonna read to us from Br'er Rabbit and he says everyone needs to be ready for bed."

"It's true," Amos said in response to Diana's puzzled look. "Ever since I can remember, when all of the cousins were together there'd be a bedtime story. My daddy used to read them, but since he died Harmon took over."

Diana was glad she'd brought something nice with her: a long-sleeved blue-and-white cotton nighty that reached the floor, and a matching robe. They had some white embroidery on the square neckline, but were otherwise both plain and modest. In short, the ideal thing for a sleepover in a houseful of people she'd only just met.

When she joined the group in the front room, there were kids in little sleeping bags all over the floor. A fire had been lit in the wood stove and the room was cozy; Diana was surprised by how much the temperature dropped after dark. Harmon had an old book in his hands, and the adults — all in nightwear — were waiting for him to start, too.

Jimmy, wearing pajamas printed with zoo animals, came up and introduced his corduroy elephant to her.

"This is Elmer. He's my elephant. When I grow up, I'm going to be a zookeeper. Maybe you and I, and uncle Amos, can go to the zoo some time. I can tell you about all the animals. Well, I'd better get settled down in my bedroll for the story, but I wanted you to meet Elmer." He was in his sleeping bag in seconds.

Amos came down to the living room and found Diana seated in a comfortable chair toward the back of the crowded room. He wore a pair of green and gold plaid flannel pajama pants and no shirt. Amos was slim-hipped and muscular, with just a scattering of black hair on his chest, and a tattoo on one of his pecs. Diana had to avert her gaze to keep from staring as she thought about how Amos had held her, just minutes ago, against that rock-solid body.

"Jimmy surely has taken a shine to you," he said. "I hope he isn't driving you crazy. He's a precocious kid, and I think he's lonely. Still, he can be a little overwhelming."

"On the contrary; he's a delightful little boy," Diana replied.

Harmon cleared his throat to get everyone's attention then. The room became quiet except for the rustling of sleeping bags.

"So, Miss Diana," Harm said, "Everyone here probably knows this but you … and if you already know, I apologize. But I've been a school teacher for a lot of years, and I can't help myself."

Everyone laughed.

"These stories were collected right up the way at the old Duparc place, which is now called the Laura Plantation. You make that *couillon* brother of mine take you, hear?

"Anyway, let's see what ol' Br'er Rabbit is up to."

Amos sat down, cross-legged, on the floor in front of Diana. Without really thinking about it, she slid her fingers into his thick, black hair … and he leaned into her touch. They stayed that way, Diana stroking his hair and Amos enjoying every second of it, until the story was over. Billy and Annie were staying downstairs to supervise the slumber party; as everyone else said their goodnights, Amos whispered "Come with me."

He led Diana out to the screened gallery at the back of the house, where they could look out at the stars without being bothered by mosquitos. He took her in his arms and kissed her yet again.

"Lady, I want you like I don't think I've ever wanted anyone before." His voice was ragged.

Diana traced the tattoo on his chest with her finger. It was a fleur-de-lis, surrounded by the words "*Un cœur Acadien.*"

"An Acadian heart," she murmured … and then touched her lips to it before tilting her chin up to meet Amos' kiss.

Amos caressed Diana's hip through the cotton of her nightdress, drawing up the hem a little with his fingers as he kissed her again.

She broke away, breathless.

"Amos, I need to tell you something before we go back inside."

"What is it, *chère*?"

"I'm not really a redhead."

Amos tried to stifle his laughter, but failed.

"I already told you, I don't give a damn about that. But don't tell Jimmy; it'll break his heart if Uncle Harm has to give back that nickel."

Diana couldn't help laughing herself then.

"Your face lights up when you laugh like that." He caressed her cheek, and kissed her again.

It was out of character for Diana to be intimate with a man she'd known for such a short time, but she was just as eager as Amos. He led her back inside and they went to her room. Flannel pajama pants and cotton nighty were soon forgotten on the floor.

Amos was a gentle lover, his mouth and hands just tracing her skin as he kissed down Diana's neck and to her breasts. He let his mouth linger there, teasing her nipples … and then further down, taking his time and getting to know her body. His tongue parted her slowly, readying her for what was to come, teasing and licking, relishing the musky warmth he found there. When she was agonizingly near to climax, Amos moved away from her and reached for the condom he'd taken from the pajama pants' pocket. Diana slipped it over his silky hardness as Amos groaned with pleasure at her touch,. Then, she guided him slowly, drawing out the moments until their hips finally touched and Amos was deep inside her. Just as when they danced, the two moved together in an ancient lovers' rhythm.

"*Mon 'tit cœur*," he whispered into her ear, his breath warm. "You feel so good, my little heart."

Diana kissed his neck, shoulders, chest … anywhere she could readily reach. Amos covered her mouth with his as his hips stiffened, and she felt a heat blossom inside her that she'd never experienced the first time with a man. Diana was no blushing virgin, but Amos touched her in a way no one else had.

Diana fell asleep in Amos' arms. Once he was sure that he wouldn't wake her, he slipped out and went to his own room, the one where he had slept as a child. He found that he didn't sleep nearly as well as Diana did; there was much on his mind.

After breakfast with the family, Amos and Diana said their farewells and headed back to New Orleans by way of the family fishing camp. Diana was not feeling well; it had taken her nearly twenty minutes to get out of bed. The previous week had taken more out of her than she'd expected. She chalked it up to the unaccustomed humidity.

However, once Amos got her out on a boat in the bayou, she found that she felt a little improved. The cool breeze that moved the water was refreshing, and the scenery was gorgeous. The flat-bottomed pirogue, with *Fyær Mari* stenciled on the back ("Harm named the boat 'Proud Mary,' Amos explained) had a small outboard motor that took them deep into the back country without having to row. The gently moving waters and variety of wildlife were so serene and restful that Diana got a second wind. Diana took several photographs, but soon she put her camera way so that she could just enjoy the experience.

"It's beautiful here, Amos," she said.

"It surely is. These wetlands contain so many kinds of birds and wildlife that don't live anywhere else. Thing is, coastal erosion is a real problem down here. The levees keep the cities from flooding, but they don't let the Mississippi bring more silt down this way. We're losing the equivalent of a football field every ten minutes nowadays. There are whole towns that have disappeared, and this bayou used to be a lot more narrow than it is now. Hell, my daddy used to say that between the erosion and the government corruption, half of Louisiana is underwater and the other half is under indictment. Some of the problem is from industrial pollution, but don't try telling that to some of the folks down here. All they hear is that good jobs might be going away, so they're willing to ignore that they can't go swimming or fishing in the lakes."

He turned the boat around and took them back to the launch.

Back in the camp shack itself, which was a two-room cabin with a bed in one room and a small kitchen in the other, Amos made love to her again. His every touch made her desire blaze even harder until, at last, both of them were exhausted and sated. They lingered over dressing again until they could no longer put off their drive back into town.

The two of them were much less talkative on the way back, lost in completely different thoughts.

When Amos dropped her off at her apartment building, he asked if he could see her for lunch the next day and she agreed.

Chapter Eight

Build time for the little things, like resting or buying foodstuffs, into your itinerary. — Diana Corbett, *Time Away*

When Diana went upstairs, she had barely finished unpacking her overnight bag when she felt so profoundly tired that she went to bed in the middle of the afternoon. She didn't wake up until the next morning, at which point she realized that what she called The Dream had not plagued her for the past two nights.

All the same, she was still exhausted. When Amos called so that they could decide where to meet for lunch, she was still in her pajamas. He could hear a difference in her voice and asked if she was all right.

"No, I'm really not."

Although she hadn't planned to, Diana ended up telling Amos what it was like to live with Hashimoto's disease. The joint pain, the exhaustion, the memory fog that made her write things down for her articles so she wouldn't forget … all of it.

"Some days are better than others, of course. But today is not so good. I overdid it this weekend, and I just don't think I can come out for lunch."

"Then I'll bring lunch to you."

Diana was surprised. The last man she'd told about her autoimmune disorder had said "So, that means you'll get fat, right?" and had broken off the relationship shortly thereafter. That had been a few years ago, before she took the job at *Time Away*. Diana always told herself that her job made it too difficult to have a relationship, but she also acknowledged that it was a handy excuse to protect herself from more hurt.

"You'd do that?"

"Why wouldn't I? Just give me the apartment number and I'll be there as soon as the restaurant is closed."

She did so, and they rang off. She managed a shower and put on a pair of yoga pants and a loose t-shirt. She wrote up her article from the weekend, talking about the sights of Cajun country, and sent it off to her editor. He would assemble all of the articles, and plug in just the right photos to create an exciting picture of her travels.

Diana was grateful that the apartment was comfortably furnished; the couch was an inviting place to lie down. She pulled a quilt out of the closet; despite the heat and humidity outdoors, the air conditioning made her feel too cold.

When Amos arrived, he had a bag from Rouses Market with him.

"I made groceries, so I can fix us something to eat," he said. "And before I came over, I did some reading about this Hashimoto's disease business. You need to tell me when you're too tired, *chère*. I won't mind."

What Amos didn't say was that "some reading" had, in reality, been a compulsive review of not just medical journal articles on-line but of support sites. He had spent almost the entire morning on his laptop, sitting in the back of the restaurant until it was time to do the accounting. Miss Julie had looked over his shoulder to see what he was studying so intently, and just nodded to herself.

Amos pulled cabinets open until he found the pot he wanted. Out of the grocery bag came chicken stock, a roasted chicken, rice, celery, carrots, and herbs.

"I thought I'd make us some soup. We can just look at a movie or something so you can rest."

It was more than Diana could have ever expected, and she started to cry. Then, she found herself telling him about the last fellow and crying even more.

"I'm sorry," she finished. "I must look a fright now."

Amos came out of the kitchen and put his arms around her.

"*Chère*, I'm not worried about any of that. That other man had rocks where his brain should have been. I'm looking at each day and taking it as it comes. No more, no less. Hell, knowing you're going home in just a little while means that's the only thing I can do." What he didn't say was how much he would miss her after she was gone.

Amos went back to the kitchen, where he found himself taking out his aggression on the vegetables as he chopped them. How dare that fool leave Diana over something she could no more help than he could stop his eyes from being brown. He shredded the chicken and added it to the pot with the vegetables and rice.

"It'll be about half an hour before this is ready," he said. "What can I do to help you while we wait?"

He couldn't remember when he had felt so protective of anyone. His brief research of Diana's ailment had been enlightening; he now knew that he had to be careful not to exhaust her.

"There's some ginger ale and root beer in the fridge," she said. "If you could bring me either one, that would be great."

"*Chère*, you need to make more groceries than that, even if you don't keep a full pantry," he said, peering at the refrigerator's meager contents. "There's nothing here but pop and condiments."

"I can only carry so much at a time, and I go to a lot of restaurants for my article," she replied.

"We need to get you one of those folding carts, then. You can write about making groceries for your story, too."

Amos poured a ginger ale over ice and brought the glass to Diana. He sat down and put an arm around her. Diana leaned her head on his shoulder and they sat in contented silence.

When the soup was ready, Amos found bowls and spoons to set the table. He also had a loaf of Ledenheimer's bread … and hesitated.

"Are you okay with this? I read that some people with Hashimoto's can't tolerate bread…"

"It's all right," she interrupted. "I promise You don't have to worry so much. I'm responsible for what I eat. I just keep the bread down to a small amount."

But I do worry, Amos thought, because you're already special to me. He said nothing, though, devoting his attention to the meal.

Afterward, they did the dishes together. Amos asked Diana if she felt like she could walk as far as Common Street with him.

"I could do that; why?"

"Thought maybe we could take the St. Charles streetcar as far as Tulane, and I could show you where I went to school."

Diana agreed. "I'll just need a minute to change."

"No need to gussy up for me, *chère*. You do what's comfortable. And take your time."

The minute turned out to be fifteen. Diana'd replaced her yoga pants and t-shirt with a soft tunic and jeans, and wore comfortable leather sneakers on her feet. Her hair was brushed and in a ponytail, and she had a small purse and sunglasses.

As they covered the few blocks to the car stop, Amos told her about going to Tulane on a scholarship.

"I stayed with Miss Julie in her attic room and took the streetcar to school. I couldn't have done it without my aunt; the scholarship covered tuition and books, but not room and board. I couldn't have gone to college at all if she hadn't offered to help. Hell, Harmon went on the G.I .bill and helped everybody else he could. In a family as big as mine, there's a lot of love to go around, but not much money for things like college. Like I said, my daddy worked on the oil rigs; we weren't fancy folk."

When they boarded the car, Amos swiveled a mahogany seat back so that he sat facing Diana. He kept up a running commentary about the historic Garden district homes until he pulled the bell cord and helped her down. Holding Diana's hand, he led her across the street to the Tulane campus. He showed her around the park-like block that housed the university, and talked about his college days. Diana took several photos of the Mardi Gras Oak, a detail she planned to include in her story. The tree was covered in beads that students had collected during Carnival parades and thrown into its branches over the years.

Finally, they sat together on a bench so Diana could rest a bit more.

"That must have been hard, being so far from home," she ventured. "I went to school right in my home town."

"Not as hard as living thousands of miles away in Chicago; you should know what that's like, with your job.

Anyway, Tante Julie took good care of me," Amos replied.
"Three good meals a day, even while she was working to
put her own sons through school in Ohio, and never a
complaint. I've been after her to retire, or at least work less,
for ages. I figured she'd listen to me after I bought the café
… but nothing doing. She's a proud, stubborn old woman."

Amos stood and offered his hand to Diana.

"Let's get you back home," he said.

Thinking of the sacrifices his aunt had made always
turned Amos melancholy. His mother was always
surrounded by family, but Miss Julie was by herself.

They caught the streetcar back to Canal, each lost in
thought.

Amos kissed Diana goodbye at her door and she went
inside. She watched from her window as he crossed the
street into the Quarter and wondered again at the feelings
stirring inside herself.

Amos had dinner with his aunt the next evening. He
told her about the outings he'd had with Diana.

"I know, Amos," the older woman said. "My sister
couldn't wait to get on the phone to tell me about how
you'd taken that young lady out to meet the family. You are
spending a lot of time in her company, that's for sure."

She got up to pour more chicory-laced coffee for the
two of them.

"I just feel so comfortable with her," Amos said. "It's
like I've known her all my life."

"I felt the same thing when I first saw her," Julie confessed. "That was part of why I didn't feel so well when I came back to the kitchen for her chocolate that first day. She looked so familiar, even though I knew I'd never met her before."

"She's the most amazing lady, auntie. Really." Amos sipped the hot brew. "I've never met anyone like her." Even as he said the words, he knew how trite they sounded.

Still, Julie thought, there was something in his eyes as he talked about Diana Corbett. Something she recognized very well indeed. Her favorite nephew was falling in love; he just didn't know it yet.

"Why don't you help me with my medicines and we'll talk some more," she suggested. "We'll have dessert afterward."

Amos had always enjoyed helping his aunt mix her so-called medicines, bottling various tinctures or mixing essential oils with petroleum jelly or sea salt in the converted garage beside the house.. All of the treatments went into blue bottles, carefully hand-labeled with contents and use. It had been one of his favorite pastimes as a boy, even as his cousins had run outside to play ball instead. It had also given him a nose for identifying fragrances — which is why he knew just which perfume Diana wore.

Tonight, the two worked side-by-side on Miss Julie's headache remedy. The older woman mixed lavender and eucalyptus oils with a dollop of petroleum jelly; once she was satisfied with the batch, she and Amos jarred and labeled it. While they worked, Amos continued talking about what he'd been up to. The Bayou Cultural Society had asked that he come in and spend several days the following month as they worked on grants for immersion schools. The visit out to Lafayette had made him realize that he needed to spend more time out that way.

And about Diana: her illness, the fun they were having, how he'd ask her to join him at the alumni event.

The one thing he didn't tell his aunt was the number of times he'd stopped in at Royal Street antique stores, looking at rings. Even he knew it was far too soon to have a discussion like that, with Diana or anyone else. Still, it had become like a compulsion for him; each store's jewelry had to be investigated in detail. He was particularly drawn to a ruby and pearl ring he'd seen in one shop near Toulouse Street.

If nothing else, Amos told himself, he could give something nice to Diana when she left in just a few weeks' time. Something to remember him by. The very thought of her going made him ache inside.

Chapter Nine

If you find yourself in sudden need of dressy attire, check out the city's vintage shops. You may just find a treasure. — Diana Corbett, *Time Away*

The day of the Tulane event came at last; Diana had found the perfect cocktail dress in a vintage shop on St. Charles Avenue. It was a deep purple brocade that went beautifully with her hair, which she swept over one shoulder like a 1940s film star. Miss Julie loaned her a pair of chandelier earrings set with rhinestones in purple, gold and green — the colors of Mardi Gras — that were just right with the frock's sweetheart neckline. Gold metallic leather pumps completed the outfit.

Amos came to pick her up in a town car with a driver. If she'd thought he was handsome in jeans, she hadn't seen anything yet; his tuxedo had clearly been made for him, and the crisp lines suited him well. He helped her into the car and they headed for City Park.

"You look absolutely beautiful, Diana," Amos said, then kissed her neck. He could smell that same heady perfume. At that point, all he could think of was how he wanted her in his bed wearing nothing but those fabulous earrings and the high-heeled gold shoes. Take it easy, *couillon*, he reminded himself. We have a whole evening to get through.

When they got to the event, Amos was filled with pride as he helped Diana out of the car. He held her hand as they went up the stairs and into the New Orleans Museum of Art for dinner and dancing. The band was better than average, and he looked forward to holding Diana in his arms for a few dances before dinner was served.

They hadn't been at the museum for long when Diana excused herself to the powder room and promised to meet Amos at the punch bowl. It was there that he ran into a familiar face from his past.

"Cousin John," he said. "What a surprise to see you here; you didn't go to Tulane! What brings you to the party? Does Aunt Julie know you're in town?"

"Amos," the other man replied, "It's nice to see you. My mother doesn't know I'm in town, and I'll thank you not to tell her. It was embarrassing enough as a kid to have her fussing around with her weird healing treatments and spying on us so that she always knew what we were up to. I don't need it as an adult."

Diana joined Amos and took a cup of punch from him. Amos introduced his cousin John Fredericks. Diana didn't see much of a family resemblance; John was soft and paunchy, and his tuxedo didn't fit well. His flyaway blond hair was poorly combed, and he seemed to have had a little more to drink than he should have.

"Nice to meet you, Diana," John said. "Actually, it's Doctor John Fredericks. I'm an ophthalmologist in Cincinnati." He seemed very proud of himself.

"It's a pleasure to meet you," Diana replied.

"Anyway," John continued. "You're right. I didn't go to Tulane, but my wife did. In fact, there she is. Kelly, why don't you come and say hello? Leave it to me to marry my nurse, eh, cousin?"

A tall, thin woman dressed in black and wearing a great deal of heavy gold jewelry, her red hair fashionably cut, turned around just then.

"Why, Amos! Imagine seeing you here. Are you going to introduce me to your little friend?"

"Certainly, Diana, I would like you to meet Kelly … Fredericks, I suppose, isn't it? You've heard my family talk about Kelly before. Kelly, this is Diana Corbett, of *Time Away* magazine."

The penny dropped for Diana; this elegant woman was the "no-account Kelly" that she'd heard so much about during their visit to Lafayette.

"Oh, you're a reporter! Isn't that sweet? And what an interesting ensemble you've chosen for the evening." She turned her attention to her former husband, speaking as though Diana weren't even there. "Really, Amos, she's so colorful that if Storyville hadn't been closed for a century I'd ask which parlor house you pulled her from."

Amos sat down his punch, a vein pulsing in his jaw. "Kelly, if you were a man, I'd ask you to step outside."

"Oh for God's sake, Amos," John interrupted. "We're not far from where the dueling oaks were; you might just as well slap someone with a glove and ask them to name their seconds."

"Stay out of this, John," Kelly said quietly.

"I'm no longer available to listen to your bullshit, Kelly," Amos said. "So, I suggest you lay off my lady friend."

Diana put her cup of punch down next to Amos' and picked up her little evening clutch.

"Amos, I'm not feeling well. Could we go? But before we do, I'd like to offer a thought of my own. Kelly, you might want to consider being a little more 'colorful' yourself. Black tends to make redheads look sallow. Good evening to you both."

Amos wasn't one to miss a hint. "I'll ring the driver and get you home," he replied. "John, Kelly. Enjoy your evening." He put his hand on Diana's waist and the two headed for the door.

As they walked away, John said "I always hated that whole coon-ass side of the family."

Amos turned on his heel.

"What did you say?"

"I said, I always hated that whole coon-ass side of the family. What do you plan to do about it?"

"If it were just the two of us, cousin, I would take you outside and beat you into the ground. However, we are in a public place, so I guess I'll just have to remind you that your mother is part of that 'coon-ass side of the family.' And that maybe you should be just a little more respectful."

"I meant every word I said."

Amos was balling up his fists when Diana put her hand on his arm.

"Let's just go, Amos. He isn't worth the effort, or the jail time. After all, the best he can do in life is to pick up your no-account leftovers. Good evening, Doctor and Mrs. Fredericks."

When they were outside and waiting for the car to be brought around, Diana started laughing.

"I'm sorry, Amos. The whole thing was just ludicrous," she gasped as the giggles died way. "She can't stand the idea of you being happy, even after all of this time, can she?"

"I'm the one who should apologize; she had no right to talk about you that way. And don't get me started on him disrespecting Miss Julie. His own mother. Jesus wept."

"I couldn't care less, really. I completely understand why your family didn't much care for her, though. What I don't understand is how ..." She stopped, realizing she was about to overstep her boundaries. "Well, let's leave that alone. You're going to have to explain 'coon-ass' to me, though."

"You don't understand how I could have married her, is that it? Well, looking back on it, I'll be damned if I know. I thought she was beautiful; she sure turned my *couillon* head, anyway. And it seemed like we had everything in the world in common. Like I told you on the way out to Mommy's place, she sure seemed willing to follow me anywhere — but only as long as 'anywhere' meant getting out of Louisiana. I'm sure she's proud to be a doctor's wife … and equally glad to have my cousin John for a husband, because he hates it here, too.

"As for coon-ass, it's a low thing that some people call Cajuns. Hell, even some Cajuns use it as a way of reclaiming. It comes from a French word that means dirty and ignorant, and it was usually applied to whores."

The car arrived then, and took them back to Diana's apartment so that she could throw a few things into an overnight bag before going to Amos' place on St. Ann. Once inside, Amos whispered his wish from earlier in the evening, and Diana smiled slowly.

"Unzip me, Amos," she said.

Under the dress, Diana wore a lacy purple bustier and matching panties.

"Well, well," Amos drawled appreciatively. "What a saucy girl you are."

Amos wasted no time in removing his own clothing before picking up Diana and carrying her into the bedroom. He placed her gently on the edge of the bed and slipped her panties off. He knelt and set his mouth to her as she laid back; his warm tongue probed deeply and sent flames of desire through her body.

Amos shifted her legs to the bed and reached behind her to unhook the bustier. He took first one nipple and then the other into his mouth until they stood in proud peaks.

Diana had been gently stroking the velvety length of his sex with one hand.

"I want you inside me, Amos," she declared as she guided him towards her.

After a quick reach for a condom from the bedside table, Diana slid it over Amos' hardness. Then, he sheathed himself in the warmth of her body, kissing her deeply as he did so. She wrapped her legs around his waist, carefully not to poke or kick with the elegant golden pumps.

The flame that Amos had started in her soon became a blaze; her body tightened around him. Amos kissed her deeply as the blaze became an explosion, followed shortly by his own body stiffening and a release so intense that it was both pain and pleasure combined.

Diana slipped out of her pumps and carefully placed Miss Julie's earrings on the nightstand. Then, Amos held her in his arms and watched her fall asleep. He had never experienced anyone like Diana Corbett before, and he couldn't imagine being with anyone else but her ever again.

Diana woke to the sound of quiet guitar playing, and Amos singing an old Van Morrison song about a girl as sweet as tupelo honey. She got up and grabbed Amos' discarded tuxedo shirt from the night before, slipping it on and buttoning it up. Then, she went into the living room to watch and listen. Amos was wearing jeans, playing with his eyes closed as he sat on the floor. His voice was soulful and rich with emotion. When he finished the song, he was a little surprised to see Diana there.

"I didn't mean to wake you."

"It's all right. That was beautiful, Amos." She sat down next to him on the floor and put her arms around his waist, leaning her head on his shoulder.

"I'm glad you liked it." He put the guitar back on its stand before changing the subject. "I need to go to the restaurant today."

"I know; it's sack lunch day. Can I come and help?"

"I'd love it if you did, Diana."

He wanted to say more, but left it at that. He called a cab for Diana after she dressed, and she went back to her apartment with a great deal on her mind. Her party dress still hung in Amos' closet, carrying the subtle hint of Diana's perfume.

Chapter Ten

Talk to the locals about what it's like to live there. You'll be amazed at what you learn. — Diana Corbett, *Time Away*

Diana spent her morning visiting various French Quarter shops and chatting with the employees; she wanted a working person's perspective on what life was like in the Crescent City, and that was the best way to get it. At lunch time, she made her way to the Bayou Café for a bowl of gumbo and then joined the employees in handing out sack lunches from the back door.

Diana also talked with the people accepting the lunches. Some of them were indeed homeless, but more of them were just getting by as the city became more expensive and income didn't go up to match. There were some whose bayou homes were under water, and who had come to New Orleans in hope of finding work years ago and barely made ends meet. Yet others viewed the sack lunch gathering as a chance to see friends.

"The Krishna Center does a nice free dinner over-town on Sundays," one older woman explained to her. "It's all vegetarian, and practically the whole neighborhood turns out for it. They even let you bring containers to take food home. Sure, you need to listen to some philosophizing, but the food and company are first-rate. No one asks questions about how much money you make, or what you believe in. Same idea as what young Mister Boudreaux does here. It's *lagniappe*, you know? Something extra for no reason but to be neighborly."

When the last sack lunch had been handed out, Felix, Diana, and Miss Julie tidied up the dining room and kitchen while Amos did the books for the day. Diana had never been part of an outreach day like that before, and she felt energized. This was nothing like ladling food onto trays in a soup kitchen; it was much more personal. She'd enjoyed every minute of it, even though she knew she'd be exhausted later.

All the same, when Miss Julie asked if she'd like to come over with Amos for dinner that evening, her acceptance was enthusiastic.

Chapter Eleven

In New Orleans, history is everywhere. — Diana
Corbett, *Time Away*

Amos walked over to Diana's apartment a few hours
later to escort her to his aunt's house. They took the St.
Charles Avenue street car, snuggled together on the hard
mahogany seats. Amos draped his arm across Diana's
shoulders and held her close.

"Just wait until you taste my aunt's cooking," he said.
"Don't you dare tell my mama, but I think Tante Julie's
better in the kitchen."

"Considering how much I enjoyed your mother's
gumbo, that would take some doing!"

When the two of them walked into Miss Julie's cheerful
little pink and white shotgun house off of Broadway,
delicious smells wafted to greet them.

"I've got jambalaya on the stove and biscuits in the
oven," the elderly lady announced by way of greeting. "I'm
so glad the two of you could come. Now, why don't you
two have a seat. I've got sweet tea or lemonade, and I've
just put coffee on. What can I get you?"

Diana sat down at the little dinette, a glass of lemonade in her hand. Miss Julie was chatting away to help her feel at home; again, she couldn't help contrasting Amos' life with her own ... and finding her own coming up wanting. She envied him, being so close to his family and with so many interesting things to do right in his own town. There was a lesson in that, she was sure.

Miss Julie brought her a photo album to look at, and Amos sat near her to tell stories to go with the pictures. There were several pictures of Amos in his college days, his black hair worn long ... and one that showed him with his head shaved smooth.

"I thought Tante Julie was going to cry when I did that cancer awareness benefit," he said. "You put money in the kitty for cancer research and they shaved your head. I never did it again, though; it made me look too much like Yul Brynner in 'The King and I,' with my earring."

"His hair was pretty as a girl's, I always said. He started wearing it long when he was in a band. Made him look like he was part Houma which, for all we know, we might all be," Miss Julie remarked as she took the biscuits from the oven. "Still, it was his head and his hair to do with as he pleased, and I couldn't argue with the cause. You know my nephew Harmon lost his wife to cancer. I expect Harmon still has the picture of Amos and Marie in the hospital, laughing and rubbing each other's bald heads. Still, it was a shock when he came home that day."

"I imagine it was!" Diana reached over and stroked Amos' hair. "I like it short like this; I have to say."

"If that's how you like it, that's how it'll stay, *chère*."

Miss Julie put dinner on the table, said a blessing over it, and they all dug in to the delicious meal.

"Miss Diana, you need to tell me about the favorite place you've visited," Miss Julie said. "I always wanted to go travel, but with two little boys it just never seemed to work out like I wanted."

"Well, I really did love London and Paris," Diana said, and then launched into some of her favorite tales from living abroad. She talked about going to the theatre, riding the subway, visiting places ranging from palaces to pubs. She even told about the time the power went out in her neighborhood and she slept wearing pajamas, robe, socks and jacket to stay warm enough. She made even the challenging parts of travel sound like a joy.

Amos listened with rapt attention; he couldn't help noticing how much Diana's eyes lit up when she talked about where she'd been and what she'd done. It was clear to him that she loved having so many different experiences and meeting all kinds of people. It was likewise astonishing that she did it while living with an illness that exhausted her so readily. Her resilience amazed him.

Miss Julie brought out buttermilk chess pie for dessert, along with chicory-laced coffee and a jug of milk. After enjoying the pie, Diana insisted on helping with the clean-up. To Amos' surprise, his aunt agreed; usually she insisted on doing everything herself. The three of them cleared the table and set about "saving the dishes."

Diana was drying dishes while Amos did the washing up. She was having so much fun with Amos and there was no way around the fact that she loved his kisses … the which he was stealing even now, if he thought Miss Julie wasn't looking.

"Amos Alcide Boudreaux, you do not have to sneak around me. You can kiss a girl if you want," his aunt said as she walked in and started putting away the dry plates and glassware. "I wasn't born yesterday, you know."

Diana put down the glass she was drying.

"What did she call you?"

"It's pretty awful, isn't it? My middle name is Alcide."

With that, Diana did something she'd never done before.

She fainted.

Chapter Twelve

Luckily, Amos caught Diana before she fell to the floor.

"Bring her into my room," Miss Julie said. She went ahead as Amos carried Diana in his arms, shooing the cats, Teddy and Timmy, from the bed and pulling back the quilt. "Lay her down here."

She pulled the sheet over Diana, who was muttering something to herself. Her eyes rolled and moved beneath her lids.

"What's she saying?"

"I can't quite make it out. It's French. Go get a couple of chairs from the kitchen. I need to sit down."

Amos put one chair on each side of his aunt's narrow bed. He leaned closer to Diana, trying to understand her words. The one word he caught repeatedly was "Alcide."

He took one of Diana's hands in his "I'm here, there, I'm here." he whispered. Concern was writ large on his face. His touch seemed to calm her, but still her eyes did not open.

"It's like she's somewhere else, Tante Julie."

"Maybe she is …" Miss Julie sat down in a chair and took Diana's other hand. "Who are you, Miss Diana?"

"I'm Evangeline," she murmured

Amos and Miss Julie exchanged looks.

"And my nephew?"

"Why, he's Alcide, of course. The man I love."

"I love you, too, *chère*," Amos whispered, surprising only himself by the admission.

Miss Julie shook her head. "I still can't see it."

"What do you mean, Tante Julie?"

"When I was a young woman, I used to be able to see things sometimes that other people couldn't if I just touched someone's hand. I can't see where she's gone, Amos. I haven't tried in a long while. The boys hated that their Mommy was 'peculiar like that,' you know? That's why they lit out as soon as they were old enough and never came back. Hated being Cajun and 'backwards,' as they called it. And even more they hated me treating people with my medicines — and maybe even more still because they worked."

"Tante Julie, I had no idea."

"Well, now you know. How'd you think I always knew when you and your cousins had been doing something you shouldn't have?" Miss Julie put her hand on Amos' arm. "Anyway, I can't think about those boys right now —not even the one who told you not to tell me he was in town. No, don't you say another word about it. We need to see where this girl of yours has gone."

"Diana, please come back to us," Amos whispered.

"It won't work, *cher*. She's someone else right now." Taking a deep breath, she continued. "Miss Evangeline, where are you?"

"Why, in New Orleans, of course."

"Is anyone else with you besides Alcide?"

"You are, of course."

"And who am I?"

"You're Monette."

With those simple words, Miss Julie could see everything.

Chapter Thirteen

New Orleans
1824

The first time Evangeline DuPre laid eyes on Alcide Devereaux, she was eight years old. Her parents always insisted that she come down from the nursery with her governess, Monette Dumonde, to say her goodnights to guest at their balls. So, with her red hair curled in ringlets and wearing a pink dress covered in fashionable slashes and puffs, she would do her duty.

Alcide was eighteen years old and at the cotillion out of a duty of his own. As the third son, he was destined for the Church ... unless he could get away, which he planned to do that very night. Still, all three Devereaux boys were expected to show up at the marriage mart balls.

Unbeknownst to their mother Jeannette, Alcide's older brothers, Antoine and Alexandre, also visited the Blue Ribbon quadroon balls. Antoine was already negotiating a *plaçage* for a pretty young woman, Natalie. Their father Edouard, of course, had his own *placée*, Heloise ... who had so far been barren.

Alcide found the whole thing a little distasteful, but recognized the necessity. He was more than a little amused at how the eight-year-old daughter of the house was already being trotted out to show her hostess manners.

"Good night, *monsieur*," the little girl said, looking up at him. Alcide was well over six feet tall, literally head and shoulders above most of the men present.

"What is your name, *petite*," he asked.

"I am called Evangeline, And you?"

"I am called Alcide. Good night, Mademoiselle Evangeline." He bowed, his dark eyes twinkling as he tried not to laugh at the whole display.

After Monette escorted Evangeline back to the nursery and supervised her prayers, she was taken aback when the little girl announced that, when she was grown, she wanted to marry Alcide Devereaux.

Monette thought for a moment about how to respond.

"He's a grown-up man already, and you are a little girl yet. Many things can happen between now and the time you debut. I don't think we need to worry tonight about who you will marry."

She tucked the girl in and took the lamp to her own room. Evangeline was definitely too young to hear about how Alcide would soon enough be a priest. And what a wicked waste that was, too; a boy that handsome had no business going for the Church.

After the DuPre ball, Alcide met his valet, a free man of color called Louis St. Pierre, behind the Devereaux house on Rampart after the rest of the family was abed. There, the black man handed him a bundle of clothing into which Alcide hurriedly changed: rough linsey-woolsey trousers, a plain shirt, and heavy brogans. A broad-brimmed straw hat completed the outfit.

"Are you sure about this," Louis asked. "I'm going to be honest with you, Alcide; I think it sounds like a bad idea. Those river men can be dangerous."

"The only thing I'm sure of, Louis, is that I have no intention of becoming a priest." He shielded a lantern so that only the smallest light showed. "I left letters inside for Mother and Father. Go home to your pretty wife now."

"I'm going to miss you, Alcide Devereaux," Louis said, extending his hand. "You're a good man."

"Likewise, Louis."

The two parted company. Alcide walked quickly to the wharf at Tchoupitoulas Street, where he had no trouble signing onto a river boat crew. The captain hoped the boy would be no trouble; regardless of the simple clothes he wore, Alcide Devereaux had the soft, white hands of a spoiled planter's son. Most likely, he'd be getting off the boat in horror at Natchez-Under-The Hill and running home to his mama and papa.

It would not be the first time that Alcide was underestimated.

Chapter Fourteen

The captain's dire predictions proved incorrect. Alcide was a quick study when it came to life on a steamship. The crew with which he signed on, the *Lafayette*, was rough and ready. Alcide learned to be quick with his fists and at the card table alike, both of which stood him in good stead up and down the Mississippi. Before long, he was the man with the red turkey feather in his hat: the best fighter on the boat. Fewer and fewer challenged him in port. His soft planter's body grew lean and hard with muscle; before long, it was easy to believe his riverman's boast of being able to lick a wild cat.

He also spent a lot of time talking to the pilot, an Irishman called Black Jack Gallagher. Gallagher knew every inch of the fast-moving river and found an an apt pupil in Alcide. He taught him not only how to read navigational charts, but how to take soundings and look for signs in the river itself. A new eddy could mean a cypress knee, a sandbar … any number of things. A pilot had to be constantly aware, in order to direct the captain so that the ship would sail safely.

The first time the boat stopped in Natchez-Under-The Hill, Alcide was appalled to see a coffle of slaves hauled from the *Lafayette*'s hold. He'd been unaware that the steamer carried human cargo.

"They've got what they call a good market here in Natchez," Gallagher said. "Captain makes a pretty penny here, damn his eyes."

"What do you mean?"

"Don't seem right to me, lad, profiting off selling men. That's all I'm saying … because I need my pay packet. So best you don't say anything, either."

Slavery was not news to Alcide, but he'd never thought about its many realities. His own valet was a free man who went home every night to his wife and received a pay packet of his own. Still, there were slaves on the family's sugar plantation; he'd just never given the matter much consideration until that day. Other friends and families among the Creoles also kept slaves, but the Code Noir laws dictated that they be well-treated and given Sundays off to do as they chose.

The people Alcide saw taken from the boat in chains had not been so fortunate, that much was obvious. Some of the men, their shirts in rags, showed scars from having been whipped. One of them was insisting that he was a free man, demanding to know what had become of his papers. One woman was trying desperately to hold her torn calico dress together at the front; Alcide could only presume she'd been violated. Perhaps, it occurred to him, by one of his fellow crew members.

Another woman was screaming for her son, from whom she was being separated. It was theoretically illegal to sell children under the age of ten away from their parents … but that didn't stop some of the slavers.

There had to be something he could do to help; he just didn't know what it was He decided to watch, listen and learn as much as he could. Then, he could decide what next steps to take.

It was also during that first trip to Natchez that Alcide was relieved of his virginity — and nearly his pay packet — in a bawdy house near the landing. Black Jack had brought him along for "a drink and a hand of cards, lad" that turned into much more. A woman calling herself Red Kate came and sat in Alcide's lap while he won hand after hand at the *veignt-et-un* table, and then offered to take him upstairs for two bits. Alcide readily accepted.

Gallagher agreed to hold his winnings, and few would cross him; he knew the boy would be rolled in the alley if the gamblers or whores thought he still carried his money. So, Alcide went upstairs and learned the arts of "dipping the wick" and "tipping the velvet" from a woman who had seldom had a such handsome young man in her crib and was determined to enjoy it for as long as possible. Alcide was an apt pupil there as well.

When he said he'd remember Red Kate always, she offered him a souvenir. She pushed a needle through his left earlobe and put one of her gold hoop earrings through it. He decided that he liked the rakish air it gave him, and so he left it there.

Chapter Fifteen

After several trips up and down the river between New Orleans and St. Louis, Alcide had worked his way up to assistant pilot of the *Lafayette*. Black Jack Gallagher had taught him not only where the bars were, which would require that the boat be walked over by any slaves on-board, whether they were in the hold or belonged to passengers, but also where the current ran fast and deep and made for quicker going.

Alcide became expert at knowing when a depth sounding was needed. When storms came through, the river changed; he had a quick eye for seeing subtle changes in the water that resulted from silt being deposited in the bed and along the banks.

Alcide found that he loved life on the river. The constant stream of new faces on the boat made every day different, although he quietly feared that some Devereaux relation would see him and recognize him. Letters from his mother revealed that the family had told their friends he had entered seminary as planned; the shame the family felt in having a son who worked with his hands was immeasurable. Jeannette said that she had taken to her bed for several days after receiving Alcide's first letter from St. Louis: "The embarrassment was more than I could bear, Alcide. I fainted dead away, and it was just fortunate that your brother Alexandre was at hand to catch me before I hit the floor."

Jeannette's fits of the vapors were so regularly scheduled that Alcide took his mother's dramatics with the proverbial grain of salt. Still, it was possible that she really had fainted this time. She'd been so proud that he was destined for the priesthood, by tradition if not by inclination; it was one of her most frequent boasts to her friends. And now, she was more than happy to pretend that he'd gone away to study rather than admit that he had run away to avoid a life he didn't want.

Jeannette had long ago discovered that denying facts she found unpleasant made her life much less complicated and thus easier. Alcide found the attitude incomprehensible, but he was long accustomed to her histrionics and, like the rest of the men in the Devereaux household, ignored them.

After their first year or so on the river together, Gallagher also let Alcide in on one of his deepest secrets.

"I buy up a nigra from time to time to free him," he confided over whiskey in the pilot house one evening. "And I know a couple of Quaker fellas who go to the auctions to do the same. They're even braver than me, though; they're the ones that escaped slaves find to help them get up North."

"I want to help," Alcide said, suddenly more sure of this conviction than anything he'd ever done in his life.

"Son, you need to be careful. It won't matter to some folks that you showed up to put out a fire if you look a lot like the people who started it, if you catch my meaning. You need to prove yourself trustworthy."

"What should I do, then?"

"Well, when we get to Missouri next, you take your money and get off this boat for good. Get you a place reading law; what this so-called underground railroad needs more than anything is a man in a law office so that he can write freedom papers. And don't you worry; plenty of folks will come to you."

"I'll do that Jack. Thank you."

Chapter Sixteen

Alcide was as good as his word. In St. Louis, he got off the boat and found himself a room in a boarding house. Then, he found a small law office run by an elderly gentleman called Daniel Harper, and offered to clerk there in exchange for reading the law books.

"I write a good hand and can cipher," he said. "I will do whatever work you see fit."

Harper would have ordinarily sent Alcide on his way. However there was something about the man standing in front of him, literally with hat in hand, that reminded him not only of himself as a young man but also of the son who had died far too young from the influenza.

"I'll give you a trial period, Mr. Devereaux. Does six weeks suit? We can revisit it after that."

"It seems fair, sir. Thank you." Alcide and Daniel shook hands on the agreement.

By the time Alcide left his employ, after nearly a year, Daniel Harper was telling people it was the best bargain he'd ever made. Those first six weeks showed Alcide to be as apt in the law as he was on the river, and before long he was being paid a decent salary. Harper lamented that he was unlikely to ever again find so good a clerk, let alone one with the oratory skills needed for the court room.

More than one St. Louis society lady set her cap for the handsome Creole, and he was regularly invited to balls and fêtes. Alcide danced with matrons and their daughters, always charming them with conversation about the latest books and theatricals. None of them were able to turn his head enough for a proposal that many hearts had hoped for, although no small number of them came to his bed. Before long he was gone, a glowing reference from Daniel Harper, Esq., naming him a qualified attorney in hand.

Chapter Seventeen

Alcide presented himself at a small law office in the newly-established town of Chicago, operated by one Aloysius Bryan. He was wearing a new suit, and had removed the earring he'd sported since his earliest days as a river man. He presented a letter of introduction, from John Gallagher of New Orleans, and asked for an opportunity to read the law and serve as a clerk. He also presented the letter of reference from Daniel Harper, attesting to his skills. Bryan found the young man on the other side of his desk well-spoken and, upon discovering that Alcide could write a tidy hand and had some experience in Missouri under his belt, hired him on as a clerk with a promise of steady access to the law books. That he got a lawyer for the price of a clerk was not lost on Bryan.

Alcide was now ready for to keep the promise he'd made to himself.

He started attending meetings at the local Quaker establishment, having learned that members of the faith were ardently opposed to slavery. At first, the quiet in the meeting house was difficult for him; the services were radically different from the pomp and circumstance of

Catholic mass back home. But he stayed, and he listened. Soon, he was invited to remain for coffee and a piece of cake ... and before long, people started talking to him. When he let it be known that he was sympathetic to abolition, he was finally approached by a congregant, John Silas, who asked for his help.

"If you can write free papers, Mister Devereaux, it would be a huge help to us. We can get people more easily into Canada if we don't have to hide them in wagons. Your imprimatur from a law office would be a huge help," the man said.

"I can, and I will."

"Now, Mister Devereaux, I need to remind you that you could get in a lot of trouble if you get caught, maybe even lose your license to practice law. You might end up in jail, or worse. If you don't feel up to the risk, I will certainly understand."

Alcide extended his hand to the gentleman in front of him. "Sir, you have my word."

From that week forward, Alcide came to Quaker meetings with at least two sets of papers in his pocket. They had been signed and sealed in advance; all that he needed to do was fill in the name so that the handwriting matched. It seemed a small gesture to Alcide, but it was of immeasurable importance to the Black people who could more readily reach Canada ... and be out of reach of the slave patrollers who could still look for them in the North.

In the mean while, Alcide continued his studies, and argued several cases in the town's court house. Aloysius Bryan offered him a partnership that Alcide accepted; the extra money he made in the offices of Bryan & Devereaux was carefully deposited against a day when it might be needed. For the time being, Alcide continued to live simply in the boarding house. He invested in a new suit of clothes and, as in St. Louis, accepted invitations to balls, fêtes, musicales, and such. Not for one moment did he regret that day, so many years before, when he left New Orleans behind; he was making a good life for himself in a booming town, and began to think more seriously about marrying than he had in the past. The society belles were more than happy to have his name on their dance cards, of course, but in the back of Alcide's mind was always the question of whether any of these ladies, in their silks and satins, would be as pleased with him if they knew about his work with the Underground Railroad.

Alcide felt that he wasn't doing nearly enough, just handing over papers and going on about his days. He consulted with John Silas again, and purchased a buckboard wagon with a false bottom. He also bought a mule to pull it, a white jenny he called Pearl. Random junk in the bed of the wagon provided his cover story. Putting on the now very ragged clothes in which he had run away from home, Alcide would help transport Black people to the next stop on the Underground Railroad disguised as a junk man. His wagon could hold a small family safely, if uncomfortably, and no one pestered a mule-skinning tinker with a red feather in his raggedy old hat. Too many people knew it meant he'd been a river tough, and that he shouldn't be crossed.

Nor was Alcide shy about using his fists if necessary. On a couple of occasions, when going through a town he didn't know, he'd park his wagon outside a saloon and go inside, just waiting on a local bully to challenge him. Win a few fights in a small town, he knew, and the people will give wide berth. He didn't care if his knuckles were bruised and cut; he'd wear gloves when he got back to town.

Thus, many of Alcide's Sundays off were spent on the road between Chicago and some of the smaller towns to the north. He felt closer to God on those days than he ever did while listening to mass at St. Anthony's.

Chapter Eighteen

Fall, 1831

"Papa, I don't want to go!" Evangeline pleaded. "Why can't I stay here in New Orleans and continue to learn from the Ursulines?"

"The matter is settled, daughter. It's past time for you to finish your education in Paris. When you return, you'll have your debut. It will be time well-spent, whether or not you're ready to believe that. A man wants a women with refinement, Evangeline, and you're not going to get as much of that here as you might think. The book-learning you get from the Ursulines is all well and good, but there is more of the world to be seen. You need to be ready to assume your role as wife and mistress of a household."

Evangeline didn't care; the only man she'd ever been interested in was long-gone from the parish. Other young men paled in comparison to the memories of Alcide Devereaux that her imagination had created; none of them stood a chance with her. Still, Papa's word was law, so Evangeline and Monette were packing their trunks. Mama was *enceinte* again, so she wasn't coming. Every pregnancy since Evangeline had failed, and the doctor seemed to think that would be the case again. Still, they were taking no risks.

"Think of it this way," Monette told the girl later on. "We'll be able to do and see what we please once we get there. Those lessons your papa has arranged are only for a couple of hours a day; you may find that you never want to come back here."

Monette also hoped that the time abroad would help Evangeline forget all about Alcide Devereaux; he was probably dead by now anyway. If God was on their side, she might even have her head turned by some handsome, rich Parisian man and they'd never come back at all.

Monette had reasons of her own for wanting to leave New Orleans and never return: reasons she had never revealed to the DuPre family. She wasn't sure whether she would ever be able to tell Evangeline or her parents that she was, legally, a free woman of color. Monette DuMonde was one of the so-called *passe blanche*: she was pale enough to pass as white. In Paris, it wouldn't matter. In New Orleans, it mattered a great deal.

It took three weeks by sea to reach the port of Le Havre, and another three days by coach to reach Paris. Evangeline barely took interest in her surroundings; she had never felt so alone or abandoned in her entire life. She was writing letters to her mother that would be mailed the moment they got to Paris, talking about the meals, dancing, and other first-class passengers they met on the ship … and begging to come home, please, as she did not want to be away from her family. Monette, on the other hand, saw the voyage as a great adventure. She had never been outside of New Orleans since the day she was born, and was determined to delight in everything.

Evangeline didn't light up again until they arrived at the home her father had rented: a townhouse in the shadow of Notre Dame. There, a butler answered the door, and two maidservants and a cook were lined up to greet them. That was the moment she realized that she would be running the household herself, and would be far from idle when her tutors were not present. It would be good for her to be busy.

Paris was very different from New Orleans. For starters, the streets were not flanked by gutters filled with sewage and filth. No one had to put down a plank to walk from the street to the banquette; Paris had sewers. For another, Paris was enormous when compared to the Vieux Carré; very few things were an easy walk from their townhouse, and so hansoms or sedan chairs were hired as needed.

Evangeline now wrote chatty letters home to her parents, and to her friend Juliette Dubois, talking about the churches, museums, and restaurants she visited. Those who knew her well could read between the lines and see the loneliness; there was no discussion of new friends made. However, there were no more pleas to come home, which was a relief. Her father was also relieved that there was never any mention of gentleman callers; he had no intention of allowing Evangeline to remain in Paris. He gave what she could only think of as conflicting messages, telling her that she was to stay in Paris as long as he intended, but not to get any ideas about remaining there permanently.

"You'll stay as long as I want you to and no longer," Michel had said. He told himself he had her best wishes at heart. Not only would she come back with an improved education, but perhaps she'd be protected from the illnesses that ravaged New Orleans on an annual basis. They really needed to do something about that disease-causing miasma, he thought.

Her father may have hoped that getting Evangeline out of New Orleans would protect her from yellow fever, but he had no idea that cholera raged in Paris. Evangeline and Monette donated food to the hospitals, taking the baskets themselves and handing them to nursing sisters through the back door.

There were so many hungry people in Paris, and not just in the hospitals. There were no pets to be seen; even the zoo animals had been killed and eaten by that time. The situation was horrifying.

Evangeline wrote to her family, asking whether she and Monette should return because of the outbreak. Her father's response was that the yellow fever was so bad that year that he could not allow it. "Stay away from the miasma as much as you can, daughter, and continue your lessons."

A postscript to the letter informed Evangeline that her baby brother had been stillborn and asked that she have a mass said at Notre Dame for his soul.

Chapter Nineteen

Paris

Evangeline's mornings three days a week were filled with dance lessons, conducted by the elderly Monsieur Delacroix; he played the piano whilst barking out instructions to Evangeline and his nephew, Jean-Claude. The dark-haired young man was a student at the Sorbonne, earning a little extra money by working with his uncle as a dancing partner for girls who far too frequently trod on his toes. Luckily, Evangeline was a good dancer and Jean-Claude looked forward to the mornings at her home.

Other days featured visits to the city's dressmakers; Evangeline's body seemed to be changing by the minute at times, as her waist became smaller and her hips and bosom more curvaceous. She also had tutors in literature and philosophy who came to the house; young women were not permitted in the universities, so the teachers came to those few homes where the girls would be educated beyond merely reading their Bibles, writing their names, and managing the simplest of household accounts.

In the afternoons, Evangeline was either paying or accepting calls ... many of them from young men who had heard that the heiress to an American banking fortune was living in the townhouse and who accompanied their mothers to meet her.

She was not interested in any of their attentions. She considered setting her cap for Jean-Claude at one point, but only because his black hair and dark eyes reminded her of Alcide Devereaux. The idea died aborning when she learned that his lady friend, Marianne, was one of the seamstresses at her dressmaker's shop. Unlike some young women, Evangeline was not one for breaking up relationships to satisfy her own wishes, dreams, or desires.

So, she contented herself with dancing in Jean-Claude's arms, during which time they also talked about his studies. Jean-Claude was quite a philosopher, and had ideas that could only be described as revolutionary. He believed in the equality of all men, and that the wealthy had a responsibility to share their good fortune with those who had less. Evangeline listened attentively, as well as asking questions so that she could learn more. The concepts that Jean-Claude shared would surely never have been brought up by the Ursulines.

One afternoon, while Monette was napping, Evangeline decided to visit a nearby tavern that Jean-Claude had mentioned was a favored haunt of his friends. He was there in the corner, talking with a group of young men. He looked up and saw her in the doorway and motioned for her to join them.

Jean-Claude introduced Evangeline to his friends who, like him, were students at the Sorbonne. They invited her to join them for a glass of beer and shared their meat pie with her. They continued talking about freedom and equality for some time.

When at last Evangeline said she had to go back home, Jean-Claude offered to walk her.

"I have learned so much from you and your friends," she said. "I have so much, and I need to use what I have to help those who have little. I will always remember the things you have shared with me, Jean-Claude."

Jean-Claude seemed, for a moment, as though he was wrestling with what to say. He would be lying to himself if he pretended no attraction to Evangeline. Still, there was Marianne ... and Evangeline would be leaving eventually.

"It is kind of you to say so," he finally responded. "I am only doing my best, in an undoubtedly imperfect way, to make my mark in the world. It is all any of us can do. One day, you will find your own best way to make your mark, and I believe with all of my heart that it will be as beautiful and amazing as you are yourself."

At the door, he kissed Evangeline's hand. "I think it would be best, mademoiselle, if we didn't speak of this where anyone can hear. It must be our secret, lest your chaperone decide that you and I are never to speak at all."

Reluctant though she was to do so, Evangeline agreed.

As she went inside, she could hear Monette still snoring. At least she hadn't been caught. This time.

She also decided that it was probably a good thing that she was not staying in Paris for good, and that Jean-Claude already had a lady friend. He was the kind of man with whom she might want to spend the rest of her life, and it was simply not possible. She was going back to New Orleans; Papa had made that clear. Jean-Claude had a life in Paris that was important to him.

Still, she knew that she would not be satisfied with any man who didn't hold the same kind of beliefs she was coming to share with the philosophers in she'd met in the tavern that day.

Chapter Twenty

Paris
June 5, 1832

Evangeline was browsing through a favorite bookstore in the *rue* Chanvriere when Jean-Claude saw her through the window. He went inside immediately.

"Mademoiselle DuPre," he said, "Evangeline. I beg your pardon for interrupting. You must go home and stay there. It is soon going to be dangerous in these streets. I dare not tell you more. Please, just trust me. Go quickly. Now."

Evangeline was so surprised that she obeyed him without question. She put down the book she'd been considering and went directly home after collecting Monette at the tea house next door. Jean Claude would not have told her to do so unless he had good cause, she reasoned. She would ask him about it during their next dancing lesson.

The following day, she learned that Jean-Claude and many of his fellow students had died as they tried to raise a revolution against the king. Their goal had been to ensure that the hungry were fed and those living on the streets had shelter. They believed that the people of Paris would rise and join them, but the people of Paris stayed home. In the end, there were thousands of soldiers from the National Guard standing against a couple of hundred students and believers. It was best and sadly described as a massacre.

Monsieur Delacroix, a black band tied around his sleeve, was the one who told her the sad news when he came the following morning for what would be one of her final dancing lessons. She went through the steps by rote in Monsieur Delacroix's arms as he counted out the rhythms he would ordinarily have played on the piano, a tear sliding down her face as she thought of all that Jean-Claude and his friends had tried to accomplish. It was a fortunate thing, she thought, that her feet could remember the dance steps while her mind was a thousand miles away.

After receiving her letter concerning the street battle in which Jean-Claude lost his life, Evangeline's father sent word that it was time for her to come home. She'd spent almost two years in Paris by that time. Her trunks were filled with the latest fashions, she knew all of the current dances, and her manners were far more refined than when she'd left New Orleans.

She'd also seen a side of life, after talking with her dancing master more about Jean-Claude's philosophies, that left her attitudes permanently changed about many things that she had taken as a matter of course when she left New Orleans. It was only upon learning that Evangeline had taken up an abolitionist philosophy that Monette finally shared her secret; Evangeline vowed never to tell a soul, a promise she would keep for the rest of her days. Still, it was time to go back to the Crescent City.

When Evangeline greeted her parents at the wharf on Tchoupitoulas, it felt as though the whole lot of them had become strangers. In many ways, that is just what had happened.

Still, though, her father thought, Evangeline's coming-out as a young woman "finished" in Paris would attract some very wealthy suitors. Why, he'd even consider one of those rough American "Kaintocks" if the fellow had enough money to properly court his daughter. Evangeline's thoughts on the matter were, so far as Monsieur DuPre was concerned, irrelevant.

If she had picked up some unusual ideas in Paris, he thought, she could surely be counted upon to keep them to herself. She was, after all, a proper Creole girl.

Michel DuPre could not have been more wrong about his daughter.

Evangeline wasted no time in addressing the issue of slavery with her father. She'd become convinced, after her conversations with Jean-Claude, that all people had the right to liberty. She did not rest until her father agreed to emancipate the two slaves they still kept upon his death or her marriage, whichever came first, and to keeping them as paid servants like Monette in the mean time. Her father's arguments that Monette was a white woman fell on deaf ears. Nor was she particularly satisfied with the compromise her father offered; wills were easily set aside when they included acts of manumission. Still, it was a start.

"You are not the girl I sent to Paris," her father said. He could not decide whether or not this was disappointing. His presumptions were falling like a house of cards, but he could see a grain of truth in Evangeline's arguments.

"No, Papa, I am not. You sent me to learn dancing and how to manage a household. And I learned those things well. But I also learned that people are not different because of how much money they have, or because of the color of their skin. We all deserve to have the same rights under the law. Besides," she wheedled, "perhaps you will look fashionable and ahead of the times by doing this. I do not think that slavery is going to stand forever."

"It is too bad, Evangeline, that you were not a son. Your passions would stand well in a room full of abolitionists, even if they were unpopular elsewhere. But I think you will not find them shared among the planters or their sons who will seek your hand, so perhaps you should keep them to yourself."

"Perhaps, Papa. Or perhaps not. Time will tell."

Chapter Twenty-One

New Orleans
October 1833

Alcide stepped off the steamship at the Tchoupitoulas
Wharf, looking around for Louis St. Pierre. The valet was
the first one he wrote to after receiving his mother's frantic
telegraph. The cable informed him that he was now the
family heir and begged him to return home.

Reluctantly, Alcide had resigned his law partnership
with Aloysius Bryan in Chicago and packed up the
belongings he chose to keep rather than sell. Law books he
had purchased, clothing … a few personal items, including
a battered hat with a red feather. He never wore it anymore,
but it served as a reminder of younger days.

As if on a whim, he'd thrown a bunch of old river
charts into the steamer trunk. If nothing else, he could
update them on the journey back. And so he had. The maps
were now as modern as he could make them. Black Jack
Gallagher would have been proud, he thought.

He soon spotted Louis, waving at him in the crowd, and
the two men heaved Alcide's trunk onto the back of the

family's brougham. Louis took the driver's seat and tapped the reins across the horse's rump.

"Madame Devereaux surely will be glad to see you home," Louis opined. "And if you don't mind my saying so, you're a far cry from the boy who ran away nearly ten years ago … so that he wouldn't have to be a priest."

Alcide smiled and stroked his mustache, enjoying anew the rakish air it gave him. It felt good to be back in the city he loved.

"A lot of things have changed," he replied as Louis made his way toward the Devereaux home on Rampart Street.

Chapter Twenty-Two

The mahogany-skinned woman, wearing an elaborate, seven-pointed blue *tignon* over her hair, put the final touches on Evangeline's coiffure that afternoon.

"Please, Madame Glapion," she had begged. "I don't want one of those ridiculous Apollo knots. All of the other girls will be wearing their hair that way, and I don't want to look the same as everyone else, tonight of all nights."

It was bad enough that Evangeline's time in Paris had delayed her coming-out until she was eighteen years old; she wanted to stand out among the fifteen-year-olds who were having their season at the same time.

"Mmm-hmm. Perhaps you want someone special to notice you?"

The older woman continued combing, pinning, and applying her curling tongs."

"Yes ... but I suspect he won't be there anyway. There's only one man I want to see in that ballroom, but I haven't laid eyes on Alcide Devereaux since I was a little girl. I thought he was the most handsome thing on two feet. He probably wouldn't remember me, even if he were in town."

"Well, you keep this under your bonnet, mademoiselle, but I was at the Devereaux house earlier today doing Madame Jeannette's hair. Maybe if you wish hard enough, a tall, dark man will come to your ball tonight. You never can tell."

"Madame Glapion, you always make the most amazing predictions . I surely do hope you are right this time."

"There you go, mademoiselle. We are finished."

When Evangeline looked in the mirror, she saw her auburn hair gently swept back from her brow and arranged in an elaborate design of ringlets streaming down the back. No wired topknot and side curl combination like all of the other girls wore; this style was perfect for her. No wonder Madame Glapion was the most sought-after *coiffeuse* in the Quarter!

"*Au revoir*, mademoiselle," she said after accepting her two-bit fee. "And keep wishing."

As Marie Laveau Glapion walked out the door, she touched the gris-gris bag around her neck and said a prayer to Erzulie on behalf of Mademoiselle Evangeline DuPre.

Marie Laveau heard talk from Black and white people alike; it was the nature of her business as a hairdresser. People talked around her all of the time, just as they did their slaves ... as though she weren't even there. Some of the talk lately was of Doctor Leonard LaLaurie; he was a young man who had come to town and married a twice-widowed woman of means. Delphine McCarty was her name, and she had demanded that the young doctor build her a fashionable home in the Quarter so that she could get away from her father's plantation out in the faubourgs near Chalmette. The house at the corner of Royal and Hospital streets was a showplace, inside and out.

The word around the Quarter was that Doctor LaLaurie had the ability to cure hunchbacks, and one of Marie's children suffered from the affliction. She had gone to the LaLaurie house with her infant son, Christophe, in her arms and been rebuffed … but not before she saw that there was much sorrow there. The slaves were miserable, and LaLaurie himself seemed unhappy. She'd heard rumors that he had another family out Plaquemines Parish way and spent most of his time there, and it was well-known that Madame Delphine had filed for separation of bed and board. To be sure, Delphine was a dark-eyed beauty, but her mouth looked cruel to Marie's eyes. It was nearly a relief to be sent on her way.

Christophe had died when he was five months old. Marie had never fully forgiven the doctor who refused to help her son. She often saw him around town, with his fly-away blond hair never quite combed and his suit never quite right. Some women might find the young doctor handsome, she was sure, but no one seemed more convinced of his desirability than Leonard LaLaurie himself. Marie had heard rumors that the doctor's father had advised him to marry a wealthy woman as no more financial help would be coming from home; he had certainly managed that the day he wed Delphine McCarty.

As for the rest of the LaLaurie household, Marie watched and kept her own counsel. Where there was smoke, there was most often fire.

Chapter Twenty-Three

Evangeline heard the murmurs at her coming-out ball before she saw him.

"Alcide Devereaux is here," Juliette Dubois squealed as she went by on her way to the punch bowl. Her blonde hair was tied up in an Apollo knot, and she wore a green-sprigged ballgown with sheer lace idiot sleeves. Juliette was always at the height of New Orleans fashion. "He's sure to be the catch of the Season now."

Evangeline wanted to be unsurprised by the news; Antoine, Alexandre, and their father Edouard had all succumbed to yellow fever that summer. Alcide had been away from the Quarter for almost ten years, coming back to help his mother and claim his inheritance. And, of course, Marie Laveau had hinted broadly at Alcide's attendance. Still, she couldn't wait to see the man on whom her childhood hopes had set. She wondered whether she would even recognize him.

Evangeline and her father led out the reel, and she found herself watching the crowd. Luckily, she knew the steps so well that no one noticed her attention was elsewhere. It was one of the skills she'd learned in Paris that stood her in good stead.

There he was, leaning against a wall and watching the dancers. Alcide was still taller than just about every other man in the room, but now he was lean, his skin bronzed by the sun. His hair was slicked straight back with macassar oil; none of those silly curls over his ears that the other men sported. He also had a thin, closely trimmed black mustache but no beard. For those things alone he would have stood out from the other men, but there was also an air of fearlessness about him that none of the others possessed. Gone was the soft, coddled planter's son. Evangeline had heard that he'd been at sea or some such before reading the law in up in Illinois among the American Yankees. It seemed impossible, but the man was even more handsome than the boy she remembered. His sharp profile and steady gaze put her in mind of a hawk watching for likely prey.

After the reel, the local boys and men started making their rounds to sign dance cards. Each of the women had a little card and tiny gold pencil tied to her wrist with a ribbon.

"Surely this is not the little Mademoiselle Evangeline who bade me good night so many years ago."

There he stood, right in front of her. His evening attire was flawless, but for the gold hoop that hung in his ear. Alcide's dancing slippers were polished to the ideal sheen; his linen was crisp and perfect. Where some of the other men layered three or four waistcoats, in what Evangeline thought a ridiculous and vain fashion, he wore two. Next to his shirt, the figured China silk was celadon green. Atop that, the waistcoat was the same figured fabric in burgundy. A garnet the size of Evangeline's thumbnail hung from Alcide's watch fob. He looked the way Evangeline had imagined the pirate Lafitte: swarthy and handsome.

"I've never seen another girl with hair like yours. Who would have guessed that the curtseying little girl in ringlets and ruffles would grow up to be such a fine young woman?"

Indeed, she had grown into quite a lady, he thought. Her powder, rouge and kohl were applied with a light hand, and she stood out from the crowd in her fine Parisian ball gown of pink silk and blond lace. The rest of the debutantes wore simple white gowns, each one blending into the next in their sameness. Evangeline was like a rose among lilies.

"You flatter me, Monsieur Devereaux."

"Not at all." He gestured for her dance card and pencil, writing his name in for two dances and the waltz right before supper … which meant they would go in together.

"I've never forgotten you, Monsieur Alcide," she blurted out.

"And now you flatter me." His smile was wry.

"Not at all," she rejoined.

The other planters' sons, and even some of the American Kaintock men from across Canal Street, hurried to sign Evangeline's dance card before making their polite rounds to all of the young ladies at the Theatre d'Orleans that evening. Even the aging Marquis Bernard Marigny, the still-handsome creator of the Faubourg Marigny resplendent in his Military Order of St. Louis uniform, tore himself away from the *crapaud* table to promise Evangeline a dance. It was Juliette, noticing everything around them in order to stow it away for future gossip, who saw how Pauline Blanque's eyes followed Alcide wherever he went, and remarked on it to Evangeline.

"She's almost twenty-four years old; she knows she'll be on the shelf soon, no matter how much money her mama and that Doctor LaLaurie have. She's set her cap for Alcide Devereaux; you can tell by how she looks at him. You'd better watch out." Juliette knew that Evangeline had eyes for no one but Alcide for years; the two had attended the Ursuline school together and were fast friends. "She'll have quite the marriage portion, between the McCarty money and her inheritance from the late Monsieur Jean Blanque. Her papa, you know. It's her last season, and they all know it. And just look at her sister, Laure, making calf's eyes at Paul Tulane. How embarrassing."

Evangeline spared a glance to the pale, thin young woman in a limp white dress that looked a few years out of date. Standing next to her glamorous, dark-haired mother Delphine, Pauline seemed almost invisible. Laure, her younger sister, was a more timid version of Delphine; she seemed to shrink from each man who appeared to sign the girls' dance cards more out of duty than desire. It was likewise obvious that Laure felt she had no real prospects with young Monsieur Tulane; no younger sister in Creole society could consider courtship until her older sister was at least engaged.

More than one of Creole gentry's sons, and no small number of their fathers, slipped through the velvet curtain that separated the theatre ballroom from the Salle d'Orleans next door. There, they met with their *plaçées* while their wives and sweethearts pretended they had no idea what was happening.

Alcide claimed Evangeline for the waltz the moment it was called, and soon they were sweeping around the room. As they passed the velvet curtain, Evangeline asked him a question.

"What do you think, Monsieur Devereaux, of the custom of *plaçage?*"

Alcide was a little surprised that she mentioned it. Most Creole women acted as though the custom didn't exist. It was, in fact, the worst-kept secret in the Quarter.

"I don't hold with indentured servitude of any kind, mademoiselle, and that is exactly what it is. Young women of color sold by their mothers into the arms of Creole men of means. My late brother's *plaçée* is now without a protector, for example. No other Creole man will have her because she has a son; all she possesses are the clothing and house my brother donated to her before his death. The law makes her a non-person, even though she is free."

"You seem rather passionate on the matter, Monsieur Devereaux."

"Passionate enough that I do not have a *plaçée*. mademoiselle. I am many things, but I am not a hypocrite. And now a question for you, Mademoiselle DuPre. What are your feelings on slavery?"

Evangeline looked around the room; nearly all of her friends' families were slaveholders. She weighed her words carefully.

"We have two slaves, and my papa has agreed to free them upon his death or my marriage — after no small amount of nagging on my part. Our servants are paid a wage, and those slaves will now be paid as well. I have just come back from France, where I had the good fortune to meet some philosophy students from the Sorbonne. Some of things I saw in Paris led me to believe that all men and women must be free in order to make their own choices in life ... so as to make their mark on the world. For, indeed, that is what each of us has been put upon this Earth to do."

Looking back, Alcide would always say that was the moment he began to fall in love with Evangeline. Her words also planted a seed in his mind that would soon bear fruit.

"And how, Mademoiselle, did you come to be in the company of these young *philosophes*? The Sorbonne's halls are peopled only with men."

"My dance master had a philosopher for a nephew, monsieur. I learned a great deal while waltzing."

"I can see that you did, my dear," he replied as the piece ended and he walked Evangeline back to her father's side. "Thank you for the dance and conversation." He bowed, and moved on to his next partner.

As for Evangeline, she went through the other dances by rote. During the Lancer's Quadrille, she and Alcide were opposite each other during their sets, which meant that an occasional *vis-a-vis* step brought them together. His partner was Juliette Dubois, who was giggling more than usual and barely attending the dance itself. Evangeline couldn't even think of her partner's name as he kept up a barrage of inane chatter during the dance. Young Monsieur Tiresome was blabbering about her beauty and how he wanted to call on her; Evangeline made all of the polite noises expected of young women and the youth was convinced his suit would be welcome. He wasn't the only one to mistake Evangeline's distractedness for agreement that evening. In fact, several young Creole gentlemen determined to have their fathers send notes declaring their intentions to Monsieur DuPre as soon as possible.

As the night wore on, Alcide made his polite rounds dancing with the other girls. Mademoiselle Pauline Blanque hung on his arm after their schottische; he walked her back to her mother and stepfather and made the appropriate bows and pleasantries. Delphine LaLaurie watched his back as he walked over to claim Evangeline for the waltz.

"Tell me, Pauline, do you think that young Monsieur Devereaux would make a good husband for you? Would you be inclined to consider his suit? He has inherited rather a large cane plantation."

The shy girl could only nod. Alcide was the most handsome man she'd seen since the family had moved to town from the McCarty plantation. She didn't care about the Devereaux place in the slightest.

"I shall see to it," Delphine said quietly.

Once Delphine made up her mind, people who crossed her seemed to face problems. Pauline herself was no stranger to this; she and Laure had both been punished more than once for sneaking food to the family slaves, whom their mother fed as little as possible. This time, though, Pauline was sure that her mother's tenacity would be to her advantage. Other peoples' free will choices did not enter into Delphine LaLaurie's world view.

Alcide, of course, was oblivious to all of this. No sooner had he handed off Pauline to her mother and stepfather than he as much as forgot her. To his surprise, Mademoiselle Evangeline had grown into a young woman with values much like his own. The obedient little girl in curls was now a glamorous young woman with a mind of her own.

When he offered Evangeline his arm to lead her into supper later that evening, Alcide took the opportunity to give her a most discreet kiss on the cheek. That he wanted more than that was undeniable, but it would have to suffice. Evangeline giggled behind her fan.

"Your mustache, Monsieur Devereaux … it prickles a bit," she whispered.

"It will be gone on the morrow, mademoiselle, should it please you," he replied, his breath warm on her ear.

Neither of them would remember what was served at supper that evening. All that mattered was the steady stream of conversation they kept up. Michel DuPre kept an eagle eye on his daughter from further down the table lest something inappropriate occur. He was completely unaware that Alcide's leg was pressed against Evangeline's through her skirts under the table, or that his daughter had no intention of asking that Monsieur Devereaux move a little further away.

Chapter Twenty-Four

The next morning, Louis shaved the thin mustache from Alcide's face, and helped him pack a bag. Alcide then drove out in a little two-wheeled gig to visit the family's sugar cane plantation downriver in Vacherie. It didn't take long for word to spread that Michie Alcide had come to visit, driving a fancy red and gold buggy with a black mare hitched to it.

The house slaves waited on the porch of the beautiful gold and blue mansion to greet the man they now thought of as their young master. He said hello to each of them, and went inside the door that led to his father's parlor *cum* office. The word went around very quickly that Michie Alcide had business on his mind.

The cooks had been busy, raiding the *potager* for fresh fruit and vegetables to make a mid-day dinner of soup and salad, which was brought to his desk along with some sliced pineapple. Alcide ate the soup while it was hot, but picked at the fruit and salad while he read some of his father's documents. The entire desk was in a state of disarray, and he spent a good part of his time organizing paperwork. At long last, he found the ledgers; it was then that he summoned the men who had managed daily operations at the plantation.

Alcide studied the plantation's books, with both the farm manager and the overseer at hand. His mother had declared herself "useless at figures" (which was probably true) and avoided the plantation at all costs. Alcide feared to find the ledgers in the same disordered state as his father's correspondence. However, the factotum, one Etienne D'Amboise, and the Cajun overseer had both kept things well in hand and the plantation had been turning a profit for some time. A vast profit, as it turned out. Alcide was now sole heir to a rather surprising fortune. The overseer, Mathieu Thibodeaux, also produced a bank book that showed deposits made.

"Not everything, of course," Thibodeaux said. "I hope you don't mind my frank speech, monsieur, but your father enjoyed his games of chance a great deal. However, he entrusted the monies to Monsieur D'Amboise and me for deposit."

Alcide wondered how much money Thibodeaux and D'Amboise had pocketed on the way to the bank. It was water under the bridge at this point, so he decided not to mention it. Things would be changing soon enough; Alcide intended to be very much involved in the operation of the plantation.

He closed the account book and asked the two men standing in front of him to sit down while he told them his plans. To say that they were surprised was an understatement, but they could do nothing but acquiesce.

"I want you to gather the workers," Alcide said at last, "And tell them I will come to speak with all of them within the next few hours. I have a lot of work to do."

"Are you sure, Monsieur Devereaux," the overseer asked. "It's *roulaison* time, and this will take the field hands away from their duties in the fields and the boiling barn."

"I am well aware," Alcide responded. "I leave it to you to notify them, whether by ringing the bell or by riding out. We can spare these people for the time that I need."

When Alcide went down to the quarters a few hours later, the overseer rang the bell and all of the slaves gathered. They had donned their best clothing; Michie Alcide had been gone for a long time, and it wouldn't do to make a less-than-perfect impression. Especially since the overseer said there would be news. Usually this meant someone was going to be sold; Michie Edouard hadn't hesitated to do that. Michie Alcide had a good many papers in his hand, too. It didn't look good, more than one of them thought.

Alcide couldn't help noticing that several of the men, women, and even children wore iron collars from which rose three inch-wide metal slats tipped in rattling bells.

"What are those people wearing," he asked Thibodeaux, "and why?"

"Well, sir, those are field and sugar barn hands," was the reply. Thibodeaux's tone implied that this was a matter of course.

"And?"

"Well, you see, those noisemakers make it easier for patrollers to find runaways. These slaves are childlike in many ways, and that includes being sneaky. If we bell them, we can find them. Your father and brothers were most approving when I shared the idea with them. The collars were all made in the smithy right here," the overseer finished. The pride on his face offended Alcide to the core.

"Then," he replied, a muscle twitching in his jaw, "they can be struck off in the smithy right here."

"Sir, I …"

"It was not a suggestion, Thibodeaux; it was a directive." Alcide was so angry that his hands shook, rattling the papers he held.

"It's downright civilized, what we did," Thibodeaux argued. "Over to the Duparc place, they brand runaways' faces."

"Have any of the people wearing those collars tried to run away?"

"No sir. It's what you might call a deterrent."

"Then I don't want to hear another word," Alcide murmured before turning his attention to those gathered before him.

Alcide looked at the assembly and collected his thoughts. This was going to be a little harder than he'd thought. Taking a deep breath, he spoke.

"As you all know, I have been away in the North for a good while now, working as an attorney. My mother asked me to return to manage our family's affairs after my father and brothers passed. I have reviewed the finances of the plantation, and I know that all of you have been working very hard. You are to be commended for your diligence.

"In my hands I have papers that … that free every one of you. I also made copies that will be given to the sheriff, so that he is aware. Monsieur D'Amboise has already ridden out to deliver the documents to him."

The ripple of surprise that went through the gathering was accompanied by smiles and hands clapped together as though a prayer had been answered.

"If you want to stay on the place, I will pay you a wage and allow you to continue using the cabin where you live for the next two years without charging rent. If you want to go, you are free to so. I know that some of you were allowed to work out and have skills that you might wish to take to town. When I call your name, please come forward to receive your freedom papers."

In the end, only a few people decided to leave and take their chances in town. Free rent for two years meant a person could put some money aside for a while. Being paid to do the same work one had done as a slave? Why, that Michie Alcide was different from any master they'd ever heard of, and what a blessing that was. More than one prayer was said on behalf of the new master, with hopes that he'd marry soon and raise a fine family, and thanking Jesus that he'd grown into such a fine man.

All of those who decided to leave were Senegambian men, woodworkers every one. Their skills ranged from building houses to crafting fine furniture. In some cases, their fathers had helped build the big house, with its thirty support beams carefully cut and numbered so that they could be put together. Alcide promised that they would leave for New Orleans at the same time he did, with Thibodeaux driving the wagon that carried them. It was the only way to keep them safe from patrollers that Alcide could think of. He was confident that Louis would be able to help find the men places to stay and worthy employment in the Faubourg Tremé, where the free blacks made their homes.

Later that afternoon, Alcide stood in the smithy. He was stripped to the waist, his body gleaming with perspiration from the heat. The line in front of him was still long, but he was determined to remove every one of those horrid collars himself. With tools ranging from metal shears to chisels at his disposal, he took his time removing rusted bolts and welded joints. The possibility of injury from removing the collar was obvious, and he didn't want to cause any more pain.

In every case, the metal had already left scarring and ulcerations on the workers' skin. Alcide was furious, but knew there was little he could do beyond the actions he was taking.

As for the former slaves, it didn't take long for word to go down the line that young Michie Alcide himself was removing the shackles. The freedom papers were one thing, but doing hard work was another. He could have let Philippe Gro, the blacksmith, do the work, after all, but he was freeing them with his own hands. The loyalty that Alcide created with his compassionate act couldn't have been bought at any price.

Alcide worked in silence for the most part, fuming as he considered that he would never have known about the abuses rampant on the Devereaux plantation had his father and brothers lived. He would have stayed in the North indefinitely … presuming that he had not acquiesced to his family's demands and become a priest, at which point he would have been just as ignorant of the situation as he toiled to bring the light of Catholicism to some frontier parish. He confined his remarks to asking each person his or her name and about their families to keep them talking while he removed the collars that both parties hated.

By the time Alcide was done, darkness had fallen. He lit a torch from the smithy fire and walked back to the house with his shirt thrown over one shoulder. His muscles were sore, and he was still angry. However, the work was now done. He ordered a bath brought to his room and he settled into the steaming water in front of the fireplace. A plate of cold meat and bread served as supper before Alcide climbed into bed.

Chapter Twenty-Five

Alcide spent the next few days visiting with the newly freed Blacks on the place, finding out what their skills were. He saw a rather large number of pregnant women, their calico dresses straining at the seams across their increasing abdomens, and some with light-skinned children in tow. The women were initially reluctant to say, but it soon became clear that Alexandre and Antoine, and even his father Edouard, had been taking liberties and left children of their own behind as slaves on the plantation without a thought. Children of color inherited their mother's status, after all. Some of those children had been sold away, despite laws saying that they could not be separated from their mothers until they were eight years old. That didn't stop determined brokers, who would lie and say that "the pickaninny's just small for his age."

The stories the women told were alarmingly similar: "He promised me a dress length of good calico." "He promised he'd take care of me and give me a house in town." "He promised me freedom." "He promised he'd bring me up to the big house." All of those promises had been false, of course. In some cases, the women had been made to lay with his brothers' carousing friends. There was little Alcide could do at that point, having already freed them all. However, he did press a few silver dollars into hands and murmur apologies on behalf of the family.

The visits had not been purely social; Alcide kept careful notes and made a log book which he showed to Thibodeaux and D'Amboise. Each entry had a person's name, their occupation, and the salary they were to receive quarterly.

"I will come out here to disburse the pay," Alcide said, "so I expect a careful accounting. Anything that these people need may be drawn from the stores on credit, and we will balance the books accordingly. If I find that you are gouging prices, or cheating these people in any way, you will be dismissed without reference. Have I made myself clear?"

Both men nodded and were excused. When they talked later, over a glass of whiskey in Thibodeaux's house, they agreed that they had not expected Alcide to be so different from his brothers ... and that they were unsure what this would mean for them in the future.

When Alcide drove back into town and told his mother, Jeannette, what he'd done, she cried, railed ... and ultimately took to her bed with the expected fit of vapors. Because the next move Alcide made was to free the house slaves under the same arrangement.

"How will I hold my head up, Alcide? What will people say when they find out we pay nigras instead of just keeping them? It's an embarrassment."

"On the contrary, Mother. The real embarrassment is telling men and women that the color of their skin is what makes them worthy of freedom. It's a sorrow and a pity that men and women should be sold like cattle, and if you can't see that today, well, I hope you see it soon."

Eventually, taking to her bed was not enough to satisfy Jeannette Devereaux; she decided that nothing would do but visiting her sister Louise in Milneburg. She packed up herself, her now free maids, and most of her belongings, leaving Alcide alone in the Rampart Street house. He promptly decided to take over his father's office space as a study and continue to live in the *garçonniere* as his elder brothers had done before him.

It was to the *garçonniere* that he repaired after his mother's dramatic departure. He wanted nothing so much as a nap.

Alcide undressed, putting his clothes in the armoire. Nothing looked like it needed brushing. Linen went into a nearby basket to be laundered later.

He unrolled the mosquito barre at the head of his bead and slid under the mesh. He closed his eyes, but sleep would not come. His thoughts kept shifting to Evangeline. He wanted her as he could remember wanting no other woman Alcide envisioned all of the ways he wanted to make love to the young woman who'd captured his fancy. He imagined parting the red curls of her sex to tease her with his tongue as Red Kate had taught him so many years ago. And then he imagined burying his manhood deep inside her.

The sheet with which Alcide had covered his nude body would soon join the other items in the laundry basket. Afterwards, Alcide was able to get the nap he craved.

When Alcide woke from a much-needed rest, he found himself in a quandary. His mother had not only decamped herself, but had taken every one of the servants. A quick view of the kitchen in the outbuildings showed not a speck of food; he wondered what his mother was eating ... and where. And with whom. It was not outside the realm of possibility that she would entertain suitors; the Widow Devereaux was spectacularly unfit to do much more than spend money. Not that this made her unusual in her circle; respectable Creole women were expected to have children, manage the household staff, and be decorative.

How interesting, Alcide thought, that Evangeline DuPre represented more than that. Her ideas, her quick and clever mind ... and there was no denying that the girl was beautiful.

Before his thoughts took him in a direction that would put more sheets in the laundry, Alcide dressed himself and walked the few blocks to Maspero's restaurant for dinner. There was plenty of time to think about the DuPre girl later.

Despite his best efforts, though, Alcide's mind kept returning to Evangeline, and the ache he had felt for her earlier in the day. After an excellent steak and several glasses of wine, he paid the check and donned his hat and coat. It was only a little further to the American side of Canal Street, and that was where he headed.

At Countess Mazzini's, on Prytania Street, the butler took that same coat and hat and ushered Alcide into the bordello's parlor. When the Countess asked his preference, he said only that he wanted a redhead. The Countess was more than happy to accommodate the handsome Creole gentleman with a partner for the evening.

On his way home, Alcide reflected that he had come a long way from his riverboat days. Then, he would have given two or four bits to a girl in the so-called Swamp … a girl with a name like Fat Mary or Railspike. Now, things were different. The young woman at Countess Mazzini's called herself La Rouge … the Red … and she was imaginative and eager. Alcide had paid five dollars for the privilege of her company, and was well-pleased with the bargain. He was sure he'd be able to think of Evangeline DuPre without embarrassing himself, at least for the next little while. He was seldom one for whoring, and preferred going to the American side of town, where he was less likely to be recognized in the bawdy house, to visiting one of the parlor houses in the Quarter.

Chapter Twenty-Six

Alcide's work in Judge A.F. Canonge's office was easy, especially when compared to being a river boat pilot. He spent most of his days writing travel documents, signing notary statements, and reading law books. Louisiana's laws were based on the Napoleonic Code, so they were different from what he studied in Illinois. It was a decent living and the funds helped at home; Edouard's gambling debts and Jeannette's spending had the town house's finances in disarray. If it weren't for the profits of the plantation, the Devereaux family would have been destitute. Alcide had paid off his father's debts, but the profit margins were going to be lower now that he was paying workers. Everything he could put into the bank would help.

He was a little surprised when the woman who now called herself Natalie Devereaux and her ten-year-old son, Henri, appeared in his office doorway. Natalie had been Antoine's *placée*; with his death, she had no protector and few young Creole men would take on a mistress who already had another man's child.

Alcide noticed that Natalie's sleeves were discreetly patched, her gloves showed the scars of frequent mending, and Henri's wrists were visible below the cuffs of his jacket. Natalie's *tignon*, the head scarf that all women of color — whether free of slave — were required by law to wear was unadorned. Most of the free women of color covered theirs with jewels and feathers, and tied them in elaborate folds.

"Mademoiselle, how can I help you today?" He closed the door discreetly behind them and offered them chairs.

"I have heard that you worked with the underground railway." Her words were blunt.

Alcide said nothing, his face deceptively calm. How had she found out?

"I hope that you can help me. Help us. I need to go away. I don't know what else to do. Since Antoine died, we have nothing. I have been unable to find another gentleman."

This was one of the many reasons Alcide disapproved of *plaçage*; the women were legally free, of course, but unless they had the skills to run a business catering to other people of color their choices were limited. If they had no family, protector, or husband and no such skills, the women sometimes came to very bad ends indeed.

"You have the cottage Antoine gave you, and the jewelry," Alcide said quietly, pulling paper and pen out of a drawer.

"Those jewels I have not already sold, yes, but neither those remaining nor the cottage put clothes on my back and food on the table for my son." Natalie's face was resolute.

"I believe, Monsieur Alcide, that if I could get North, we could pass. Seven of my eight grandparents were white, monsieur."

He looked at the two very carefully and nodded. "Yes, I believe you could."

Alcide consulted a book and then started writing, first on one sheet and then another.

"You are now Natalie de la Vega, a Spaniard's widow. Your son is Henri de la Vega. Sell the house and the jewelry; I'll help you." He handed the identity papers to Natalie. "These documents will help you make your way North; keep them safe on your person. At the risk of being indelicate, putting them under your stays would be the best thing. As soon as you leave this city, take off your *tignon* and never wear it again."

He also wrote a draft against his account at Michel DuPre's bank and gave it to her with a note for the clerk giving permission for Natalie to withdraw the funds. "Please, take this as well. I wish I could do more."

While he appeared calm, Alcide's stomach was in knots. Forging papers like these, saying free people of color were white, was a serious crime. And yet, as when he had done the same for the Underground Railway, it was a risk he was willing to take.

He showed them out of the office, a prayer for their safety offered up to a God in whom he was not sure he believed.

Prayers, of course, were not enough. When Alcide left his office for the day, he stopped by the undertaker's and bought a dress length of black bombazine. With the package tucked under his arm, he walked over to the little cottage where Natalie and Henri lived and presented himself at the front door.

He was pleased to note that Natalie was not wearing her *tignon*; her hair was arranged in a crown braid. She looked lovely, if tired. He could see why his brother had been attracted to her.

"You need to use this to make a dress, and make sure you have a mourning veil," he said to Natalie as he handed her the material. "I'll have documents drawn up authorizing me to rent the house rather than selling it; I will send you the income care of Aloysius Bryan in the Town of Chicago. I have a letter of introduction here."

He took a document out of his pocket and put it on the table. "I will drive you to the train myself the day after tomorrow. I am sorry for the short notice, but it occurred to me that you might wish to leave sooner rather than later."

"Monsieur, I do not know how I can ever thank you."

"By making a life for yourself and my nephew, Madame de la Vega." Alcide's smile was wry. He collected his hat. "I will see you soon."

By the time Alcide was out the door, Natalie had opened her pattern books. Two days to make a dress and pack even a small household meant wasting no time.

Chapter Twenty-Seven

When Alcide left Natalie's home, his mind was already on the ball that he planned to attend that evening. He greatly hoped that Mademoiselle DuPre would honor him with further dances. He had been no stranger to courtship in the Town of Chicago, but no one had ever captured his attention like Evangeline. When he got home, he went into his mother's bedroom and opened the jewelry box that she kept there. The ruby ring that had been her engagement jewel still held pride of place, as he had hoped. He wrote a letter to his mother in Milneburg, explaining that he had met the woman he hoped to marry and asking for not only her blessing but permission to use the ring his own father had given her. He sent Louis out to post the letter before he lost his nerve.

The next letter he wrote was to Louis, authorizing him to move those freed men from the plantation who might still need a place to stay into the little cottage and to act as his agent in collecting a modest rent from each. It was an elegant solution, even if Alcide did say so himself.

That evening at the Theatre d'Orleans, Alcide penciled his name in for every waltz on Evangeline's dance card. Let the other Creole bachelors and American Kaintocks have the reels, schottisches, and quadrilles; he and no other would hold Evangeline in his arms.

"Might I call upon you, mademoiselle," he asked during one of those dances. "If it pleases you, I could come in two days' time." He saw no need to mention the reason for his delay, and Evangeline did not inquire. It might look unseemly if she were so eager as to ask for an earlier visit.

"I thought you might never ask," Evangeline responded. "I would be delighted if you did. You should send Papa a note to make it formal, of course."

Other men asked the same question that evening; all of them were politely rebuffed with an explanation that she was flattered, but her affections were otherwise engaged.

Thus began the ritual of Creole courtship, in which Alcide visited the DuPre household for tea, supper, and card parties. There were always chaperones present as Evangeline's family got to know the man whom their daughter had adored since childhood. He was a successful lawyer, heir to a sugar cane plantation, and a Creole. He'd been away and hadn't intended to inherit; thus, him choosing a profession other than the family's cane business was a matter that could be overlooked. Young Monsieur Devereaux was all that the family might want for their daughter, and it was greatly hoped in many hearts that a proposal would be forthcoming.

Their hopes were confirmed when Alcide began talking about the sugar cane plantation. His mother would be keeping the town house, but Alcide felt strongly that the plantation needed someone other than the overseer and the factotum to run the place on a day-to-day basis. He sensed Evangeline's reluctance to be so far from town and her family, but eventually got her father to allow a visit so that she could see whether the place was agreeable to her.

"In due time, I could be persuaded. Her maid will go with her, of course. We can't have Mademoiselle Evangeline unchaperoned out there."

"Of course, Michel," Alcide concurred. "The proprieties must be observed."

Pauline Blanque had noticed Alcide coming and going from the DuPre house, but told herself it was because he was an attorney and Michel DuPre was a banker. Surely it was all business meetings concerning the Devereaux's sugar business. Besides, her mother had promised to speak with Alcide … and that meant it was going to happen. Delphine always kept her promises.

Chapter Twenty-Eight

March 1834

Alcide waited impatiently for the DuPre family to enter the Theatre d'Orleans for what would be the last ball before Lent. He had paced the floor for at least half an hour, trying to calm his nerves. His mother's letter from Milneburg had given him the answer he most desired, and now he needed to take the next step.

When Michel DuPre came in with Evangeline on his arm, it took every bit of Alcide's self-control not to run over to greet them both. Instead, he walked with such steely resolve that Evangeline could only think of a panther stalking its prey. She smoothed the blue silk skirt of her ballgown and tried to appear nonchalant.

"Monsieur DuPre," Alcide said, shaking hands with the gentleman at last. "I pray that you will grant me a few minutes to speak with your daughter alone."

"But of course. I am sure she would enjoy some punch. Wouldn't you, daughter?" Michel was certain that the moment they'd all been awaiting was at hand.

Evangeline took Alcide's arm. "I suppose I would, come to think of it. Please, let's walk together, Monsieur Devereaux."

"Mademoiselle Evangeline, I find that I cannot stop thinking of you. I never fail to enjoy our conversations, and we seem to be of one accord on many matters that are important to me. I wonder, Evangeline, if you would do me the tremendous honor of becoming my wife."

There. It was out in the open. He watched his intended with an intensity that would have frightened a lesser woman.

For a moment, Evangeline was silent. She couldn't quite believe what she'd heard. Then, it all sank in.

"I will, Alcide. Oh, yes. I will." She smiled up at him. "If you must know the truth, I set my cap for you when I was but eight years old and my parents made me bid you goodnight. I told Monette that night that I would marry you when I grew up. And now my wish has come true."

"If we weren't in the ballroom with everyone watching, I believe I would pick you up and swing you around for joy," he smiled. "But now, I must also arrange things with your father. You have made me the happiest man alive, Evangeline."

Michel DuPre watched as Alcide Devereaux kissed his daughter full on the mouth, and smiled to himself. It was a good thing he'd sent her to Paris, he thought. Otherwise, how on earth would she have attracted the attention of the

Devereaux heir? Michel viewed the match, to which he would of course agree, as a personal triumph.

Alcide stood in the door of Michel DuPre's study, shaking hands with the older man.

"I am glad we could come to terms, sir. I will come with my man to deliver a trousseau for Mademoiselle Evangeline," he said, referring to the basket of lacework and jewelry that was each Creole girl's wedding gift. "Let us see the notary tomorrow morning. I will arrange it with Judge Canonge."

He collected his hat from the butler and departed.

Evangeline, who had been standing at the top of the gallery and, frankly, eavesdropping, ran downstairs to hug her father.

"Papa, I can't thank you enough! All of my dreams are coming true!"

"Lest you forget, daughter, you will soon be the mistress of a plantation. You'll need your nose out of your books and into running a big house soon. There is more to it than you can imagine. You will have servants to manage, as well as the kitchen and medicine cabinets. However, I believe you are more than equal to the task."

"Papa, with Alcide to teach me, I believe I can do anything!"

When the basket arrived, as promised, Evangeline and Monette looked at every piece together. Of course, most of the jewelry would have to wait until they were married, but Alcide himself put the engagement ring on her index finger in the French fashion. The gold-set ruby, surrounded by pearls, sparkled on her hand.

"I will call on you tomorrow, my love," Alcide said to Evangeline. "We can go for a drive." Now that they were engaged, the couple could go anywhere they wished together without a chaperone.

Chapter Twenty-Nine

As promised, Alcide arrived the next morning to take Evangeline driving. The buggy was freshly polished, and his black mare was in the traces.

"You surely do look lovely in that dress, mademoiselle," he said as he helped Evangeline onto the buggy seat next to him. While she settled the skirts of her new peach and gold day dress, with its lace pelerine and smock-shouldered sleeves, around her, Alcide flicked the reins across the mare's back.

"I thought we might ride out to Carrollton and back," he said. "Just enough to spend some time alone together for a change."

Evangeline tucked her lace-gloved hand into Alcide's elbow. "Perhaps you could talk to me about the plantation. Papa says I'll be in charge of the house. I learned something about that in Paris, but it was so general. I want to know what your place is like."

So, Alcide outlined how the plantation worked. The *roulaison*, cane harvesting, had been over for a few months and a new planting had gone in. He explained how each planting could be harvested three times, and outlined the entire process of cutting, boiling, and reducing the cane down to molasses and three types of sugar.

He also told her that he had freed the slaves shortly after their first conversation at the ball, and that the people who worked the dangerous jobs were now being paid to do it.

"Because every step of it can be treacherous, *chèrie*. The cutting involves huge cane knives. The boiling? Well, all of that hot sugar can burn right through to the bone if it spills on a person. Make no mistake, it is a hard life for the people who do this job. I am glad to pay them for it, for they take on risks that I do not."

He did not tell her about the hours he spent removing belled collars from people's necks. It was more than she needed to know just then.

Alcide stopped the buggy under a tree in a little park. He untied Evangeline's bonnet ribbons and set her hat aside before taking her in his arms. His kiss was ardent, his tongue pressing past her teeth. Evangeline's response was enthusiastic, and she felt the first flickering of real desire. After a few moments, Alcide broke off the kiss and handed Evangeline her bonnet.

"Best you put that back on, my dear." He shifted uncomfortably. "I should have been more careful, but you looked so beautiful."

"Do not apologize, my love," she replied as she tied the peach-colored ribbons under her chin. "I will look forward to more of your kisses."

Evangeline moved closer to Alcide so that their hips touched on the buggy seat. He flicked the reins a little and the mare stepped out again for the return trip to the Quarter. Alcide talked further about the plantation, doing his best to ease Evangeline's fears.

"Besides," he concluded before changing the subject, "You were very brave about living in Paris. I should think that a mere fifty miles would be nothing compared to living across the sea."

It was a perspective Evangeline had not yet considered, and one that made sense to her.

"I presume I'll be able to bring Monette with me?"

"I don't see why not," Alcide replied. "I'll speak with your father. There's no reason I can imagine that would prevent you having the maid of your choice."

Alcide drove back to his house on Rampart Street, where he deposited the coach and horse with a groom and then took Evangeline walking on Rue de Levee before taking her home. They bought callas from a vendor and ate while they strolled and chatted. All too soon, it would be time for Evangeline to return home.

Chapter Twenty-Nine

Along the River Road
Mid-March 1834
Lent

The servants at the Devereaux plantation were lined up in front of the embracing staircases when the coach arrived. Alcide stepped out first, helping Evangeline and then Monette down. Louis followed; he and a couple of the other manservants set about getting trunks down and taking them into the colorful house. Alcide went up the left side of the staircase and Evangeline the right, meeting at the top as was customary.

"Your mother has already arrived," Mathieu Thibodeaux informed him. "She has taken the blue bedroom."

"Thank you, Monsieur Thibodeaux. This is my fiancée, Mademoiselle Evangeline DuPre, and her maid, Monette DuMonde. Please have one of the inside staff see that they are given the green bedroom. I will take my father's old room."

Turning to Evangeline, he said, "Please go ahead; I will come to see you after you've had a chance to settle in." He kissed Evangeline's upturned cheek and they went in through separate doors in accordance with the custom.

The Black maid who led them to the green bedroom introduced herself as Suzette; "I'm Missie Jeannette's maid when she's here, and I also keep the medicine cabinet. I'm to do for you as well if you need," she said.

"Thank you, Suzette. I appreciate your kind offer. I am sure you will be a huge help to me, as I don't know the first thing about plantation life. I look forward to learning from you."

Suzette was surprised by Evangeline's response. Most white women didn't think Black people had anything to teach them, in her experience. It looked to her as though Michie Alcide's bride-to-be was just as unusual as the young master himself. Even though free, the blacks on the Devereaux place still thought of Alcide just that way.

As Evangeline and Monette entered the house, Alcide invited Thibodeaux into the men's parlor.

"How is it that my mother is here just in time for Mademoiselle DuPre's visit?"

"Well, monsieur, upon receiving your letter I wrote to Madame Devereaux in Milneburg and told her of your plans. She decided that she needed to come out and meet your future bride. If there's nothing else, sir, I need to get back to my work."

159

"Very well. Thank you."

Alcide was left wondering how it was that Thibodeaux knew his mother had been in Milneburg.

Before too long, Jeannette let herself into the office where Alcide was reviewing paperwork and correspondence. She was dressed in the height of mourning fashion, her crepe dress leaving black smuts everywhere she sat. Jet and diamond jewelry offset her gown.

"Alcide, my dear," she began, sitting on a chair next to the desk and smoothing her dark hair. "I am so looking forward to the noon meal and formally meeting my daughter-in-law. I remember seeing her at the balls, of course; a pretty little thing. Tell me; what made you set your cap for her?"

"Her ideas are in accord with my own, Mother. She has a good mind and a good heart. I think the match is advantageous on both sides, and that you will be pleased with my choice."

"Her ideas? Is she a radical like you, then?"

"If you call believing that slavery is an abomination radical, then I suppose she is. She finished her education in Paris, and has studied a great deal of philosophy concerning the rights of men."

"Oh, dear. A bluestocking then? Oh, Alcide. Surely this is not the kind of person you want to be the mother of your children? I may have to take to my bed before all is said and done."

Alcide put down the papers he had been reviewing and looked his mother directly in the eye.

"There is no other woman who would suit me so well, madame. Let this be the end of such words between us."

"I ... I feel of fit of vapors. I think I will retire. I shall see you at the noon meal."

"How convenient, madame," Alcide murmured as his mother swept out of the room and closed the doors behind herself.

It was only after Jeannette had been gone for a few minutes that Alcide realized he hadn't asked how Thibodeaux had known she was in Milneburg.

The noon bell called everyone to dine; the cooks were sending young boys up the Whistler's Walk with steaming covered dishes as fast as their legs could go.

Jeannette took her accustomed place at the foot of the table, with Alcide in his father's place at the head. Servants placed two soup tureens on the table, one at either end. Evangeline was shown to a seat at Alcide's right; he held the beautifully carved and upholstered chair out to accommodate her. In one corner, a young slave boy in livery pulled the punkah fan cord to keep the flies away.

"I'm sure you understand, Mademoiselle DuPre, between my mourning and this Lenten season, our table is lighter than usual," Jeannette said. "We have turtle soup, but have left out the sherry. We also have bread soup in vegetable broth. Our next removes will have lettuces and two types of fish: trout and *sac-au-lait*. For dessert, there is pineapple to welcome you to our home. I hope this meets with your approval."

"It will be delightful, and I thank you for your graciousness. It is very kind of you to invite me to see the plantation. Coming from town as I do, I am unaccustomed to the country. It is lovely here."

The niceties having been dispensed with, Alcide began serving the bread soup from his end and Jeannette served the turtle. Conversation turned to the news of the day, and before long the pineapple slices were on everyone's plate to enjoy.

For Evangeline, despite the polite smile she wore, the experience was dreadful. How on earth would she manage a household like this? Nothing she had studied, either with the Ursulines or in Paris, had prepared her for so many servants and such a large home. She felt like the worst sort of imposter; only her love for Alcide made her determined to succeed. Otherwise, she would have turned tail and run home without ever unpacking a single trunk. She almost hoped her future mother-in-law would have a whole pineapple sent with her breakfast tray so that she would be spared a lengthier visit.

As for Jeannette,, she was determined to test Evangeline's mettle. Jeannette hated the country for the most part and longed to return to town. However, she knew how much responsibility a plantation mistress had, and she needed to know that Alcide had chosen well. There was no denying the girl was a beauty, although she'd have to wear a bonnet everywhere she went; that fair skin of hers would burn and freckle, and that was no good at all.

She could certainly keep up her end of the conversation, though; she was well-read, and seemed to keep abreast of the issues by reading the newspapers. That was unusual in a woman, but Jeannette could see why Alcide would find it attractive. He'd never cared for the empty-headed girls who threw themselves at him in his youth — until they learned he was meant for the priesthood, of course. There was no reason to believe his attitude about intelligence had changed.

Jeannette's greatest hope was that Evangeline had not inherited her mother's unfortunate predilection for losing pregnancies. All of Creole society knew about the many stillbirths that had stricken the DuPre household over the years. Alcide was the only heir remaining; there was no way Jeannette would allow the cane plantation to go to one of the cousins out in Milneburg. Alcide needed sons.

She returned her focus to something Evangeline was saying about her days in Paris and nodded politely.

"That sounds fascinating," she said after sipping at her turtle soup. "Do tell us more."

Chapter Thirty

Alcide stood on the back gallery of the men's wing, smoking a slim black cheroot. He was restless, knowing Evangeline was just on the other side of the house. He pondered whether he should ask her to his bed before the wedding, especially with his mother liable to notice.

His mind was made up as he noticed Jeannette, a shawl over her white night rail, making her way across the lawn in the dark. She was headed straight for the overseer's house.

Far be it from Alcide to deny his mother the comfort of male company. At least he now understood why Thibodeaux knew so much about his mother's coming and goings. He wondered briefly how long the affair had gone on and decided he didn't care. His father had Heloise; his mother had Mathieu. And now she was out of the house.

He stubbed out his cigar and left it in the brass ash tray before going back inside.

Alcide walked through the parlors until he stood outside the green bedroom. He considered that Evangeline might reject his overture, or even be so insulted that she broke their engagement — which would be scandalous in and of itself because the banns had been signed and would be read on Easter Sunday. Yet, the ache to hold the young woman in his arms — and more — was overwhelming.

After a few minutes' hesitation, he tapped on the door. Evangeline cracked it open.

"Monette, is something wrong? Oh!" She recovered quickly. "Alcide, what is it?"

She picked up a wrapper and put it on as she stepped into the parlor. Her auburn hair streamed down her back; Alcide longed to bury his fingers in it.

He put one hand gently under her chin and tipped her face so that he could kiss her. Evangeline's response was ardent and enthusiastic.

"Will you come with me?" he asked quietly. "I will understand if you say no."

"I will, Alcide," she replied, and he led her back through the parlors to the men's wing.

While Alcide closed the door behind them, Evangeline sat on the stool next to the tester bed. She knew what she was doing, coming with him to his bedroom. Still, there was a part of her that said she was wrong to be there before their marriage.

"If you change your mind," Alcide said, seeming to read her thoughts, "I will accept that."

"No," she said. "I want to be with you. Please, kiss me again."

She stood up and Alcide took her in his arms. He kissed her cheeks, her throat … and succumbed to the urge to plunge his fingers into that auburn mane.

At last, he helped her up onto the bed and he undressed. Evangeline had never seen a nude man before, and she thought his body was beautiful. She made to slip out of her night rail, but Alcide stopped her.

"Lie back on the edge of the bed with your legs over the side," he said quietly.

Once she was in position, he slipped the night rail up over her thighs. Sitting down on the stool, he leaned in and, gently parting the russet curls there, he set his mouth to Evangeline's sex. Everything Red Kate had taught him about "tipping the velvet" so many years ago, he applied to Evangeline. She tasted warm and musky and clean. Alcide devoured her with his tongue, lapping at her like a cat. Evangeline writhed on the bed, trying not to cry out in pleasure.

Alcide stood up and rubbed his hardness against her moistened mound.

"There is every chance that this will hurt," he said, rubbing his thumbs on her nipples until they hardened. "I will be as gentle as I can."

He moved Evangeline's legs over to the mattress and joined her there. He kissed her, gently at first, and then fervently as he rubbed himself on her wetness again. Then, slowly, he slipped inside her. His breath warm on her ear, he whispered words of love as he pressed past the resistance he felt. A little tension on Evangeline's part, but not a sound other than her brief intake of breath … and then two began to move together.

Evangeline's mother had told her that "the marital act" was something women endured for the sake of children. She had never made it sound like anything near pleasurable. Yet, Alcide's mouth, hands, and body had aroused her in ways she could not have imagined. The way their bodies fit together felt beautiful. She put her arms around Alcide, stroking his hair with one hand and his shoulder with the other.

"It feels so good," she whispered, still a trifle wary of being caught.

"It is supposed to, my love," was the response just before Alcide stiffened in release.

They stayed together in his bed for a while, kissing and whispering, before Evangeline got up and went back to her room. Just as in Paris, she could hear Monette snoring in the adjoining servant's room. No one but Alcide would ever know that she was not a virgin on her wedding night.

Chapter Thirty-One

After a light breakfast of *café-au-lait* and rolls, Alcide offered to take Evangeline riding so that she could see the plantation at work.

"I haven't ridden since I was a little girl," she confessed.

"Well, I'm sure we can find a quiet horse for you. You'll need to get accustomed to riding out here; the nearest neighbors are more than a mile away. Besides, it will be good exercise for you. Meet me in the front parlor in an hour and we'll ride out."

Alcide was true to his word; a quiet grey mare awaited, with Jeannette's side saddle on her back. Alcide helped Evangeline mount and then swung his long legs easily over his favorite black Arab mare.

"We'll keep to a walk today," Alcide promised. "It will take longer, but I want you to see the whole place. You'll be mistress of this entire plantation, and you should know it as well as I do. I will show you the books later."

They rode single-file down the narrow paths between the cane rows, out to the sugar sheds, two-family cabins where the former slaves lived, and around the outbuildings. Evangeline had many questions as they stopped near each area; Alcide was glad to see her take an interest.

"Do you think I could have a little school house?" she asked eventually. "I would like to teach the children to read and write."

"It's illegal to teach blacks to read and write now," Alcide said quietly. "As a lawyer, I have to say that. As the master of this place, I can tell you that nothing would make me happier than if you did so. The ability to read and write is crucial for all people. Once we are wed, I will announce that those who wish to send their children to school may do so. We will work out the particulars before then."

He reached across to take Evangeline's hand, and raised it to his lips. "I could not be more proud of you than I am at this moment, my love. It is because of you that I have freed the slaves here, you know. You and I are of the same mind on so many things."

Evangeline blushed under her broad-brimmed hat. She was unaccustomed to such fulsome praise.

"It's time we rode back," Alcide said, turning his horse around. "I am sure that Mother needs to preside over luncheon again today, and it is better if we let her. She'll grow bored and go back to town before we know it."

As Alcide predicted, Jeannette grew weary of country life in fairly short order. She took her leave of Alcide, Thibodeaux, and the servants a few days later and rode back to New Orleans. Before departing, she confided to Alcide that she was pleased with "the DuPre chit," and that she believed she would be an asset to the family. She gave him her key to the medicine cabinet, so that he could pass it on to Evangeline. It was the surest sign of approval that Jeannette could give.

With his mother out of the house, Alcide did not hesitate to invite Evangeline to his bed whenever she wished to come. More often than not, she tiptoed through the parlors as soon as Monette was asleep. Despite her mother's assertions, Evangeline enjoyed Alcide's lovemaking and looked forward to their wedding; after that, there would be no more need for subterfuge.

Chapter Thirty-Two

New Orleans

On Easter Sunday, Evangeline joined Alcide at his home parish church, St. Anthony of Padua, on Rampart Street. The rest of her family went to St. Louis, as usual. Delphine LaLaurie marked the DuPre girl's absence, mentally upbraiding herself for hoping Evangeline was ailing Such thoughts were inappropriate in church, no matter how little she cared for religion.

Delphine's mind, as always, was on everything but the Mass. She held her rosary and kept a placid look on her face but she was thinking about her unsatisfactory correspondence with Alcide Devereaux. She had written several times asking to speak with him concerning Pauline. His response had been a polite declination, every single time.

It was thus somewhat surprising to hear Père Antoine actually say Devereaux's name. Beside Delphine, Pauline Blanque stiffened as the banns were read, announcing the engagement of Alcide Devereaux and Evangeline DuPre, as confirmed by the notary in Judge A.F. Canonge's office.

That was why the DuPre girl was absent, Delphine realized; she was hearing her banns at St. Anthony's, where she would soon enough be a parishioner herself.

Silent tears streamed down Pauline's wan face. Delphine tugged a handkerchief from her cuff and passed it to her daughter.

"Do not make a spectacle of yourself," she whispered. "You know better. I brought you up better than that. Have some dignity." If they hadn't been in church, Delphine might have slapped her.

Pauline did not know which she feared more: being forever on the shelf, or her mother. She dried her eyes and tried to keep her inner turmoil from showing on her face.

After all, Père Antoine could have been talking about a different Alcide Devereaux. Surely that must be the case. A cousin, perhaps; so many families used the same names. Surely.

The first night that Evangeline and Alcide appeared at the Theatre d'Orleans unchaperoned, Pauline Blanque burst into tears and ran from the room. No proper Creole girl appeared unescorted in public with a man who was not her fiancé, which meant that Pauline's hopes were indeed dashed.

Delphine, of course, knew exactly what was going through her daughter's mind. She also noticed a different attitude in Evangeline. There was a look in a woman's eyes that could not readily be described, but said that she was no longer innocent of a man's touch. Delphine's eyes had held that look since her first marriage at age fourteen. Perhaps Alcide had had his way with the DuPre girl, but that didn't mean he'd accept it if another man did. She watched the young couple dancing together, the ruby ring flashing on Evangeline's hand, and plotted her revenge. No one thwarted her plans.

Chapter Thirty-Three

April 9, 1834

Delphine LaLaurie called on the DuPre household, seeking a visit with Evangeline.

"I understand that Monsieur Devereaux and your father met with the notary last month. Congratulations to you on such a splendid match," she said.

Evangeline smiled, and opened the elaborate, mother-of-pearl fan that was part of her trousseau. "I think I fell in love with Alcide when I was eight years old and saw him at one of my parents' balls. I am the luckiest girl alive."

"Well, I am just delighted for you. You must come over this evening and play cards with my daughters and me; Doctor LaLaurie is going back up to Plaquemines Parish, and I will be so bored. Now that Lent is over, I want to have card parties all of the time. We'll play a few hands of *bourré* and have supper. Do say you'll come. I'll leave the plank out for you."

"I would be delighted," Evangeline agreed, and the plans were set.

Delphine left the DuPre house with a smile on her face that promised disaster. She could hardly wait to tell Pauline that Alcide Devereaux was as good as hers.

Marie Laveau saw Madame LaLaurie leaving the DuPre house, and did not like the look on her face. She knocked at the back door and begged to see the young miss, but was denied. She went back to her little house on St. Ann Street and dictated a note to Monsieur Devereaux, care of his law office on Royal Street. Few knew that Marie could neither read nor write. Luckily, her neighbor's son could do both, and he was always happy to help. After he read back the letter, expressing Marie's concern for Evangeline's safety, he was sent in search of the young attorney. Marie could only hope that he would see her letter in time.

That evening, Evangeline walked up the plank that covered the gutter outside the LaLaurie house and knocked at the French doors there.. She was wearing one of her favorite dresses, a green and pink dimity print with fashionable *gigot* sleeves and a fine lace pelerine. A young female slave opened it, her eyes downcast, and gestured for Evangeline to come in. Pauline Blanque was waiting to greet her.

"*Maman* will be along directly," she said. "We are all just so delighted for you. Come along out of my bedroom;

we'll go to the parlor. Leave your pattens here; the girl will clean them. Leave your bonnet, too."

If Evangeline noticed the uncanny echo of Delphine's words from earlier in the day, she didn't pay much attention.

"It's so kind of your mother to invite me for an evening of cards. I enjoy playing, and I'm pleased to have a chance to get to know all of you better. I see you at the balls so often, and I think we should be friends. I knew Laure at the Ursuline School before I went to Paris."

"Did you." Pauline made it sound like a statement rather than a question.

"Yes. We weren't particular friends; I was closer to Juliette DuBois. But that is a situation I should very much like to remedy." Evangeline meant every word she said; she saw no need to dissemble.

Pauline's relief upon her mother's arrival was palpable.

"Mademoiselle Evangeline, thank you so much for coming tonight. Let's go through to the parlor; I have a table set up for us to play."

Evangeline followed Delphine through the richly furnished house until they came to the parlor. Everything in the house seemed to be of the highest quality, from the silk wall covering to the heavy velvet drapes that pooled on the floor in the latest fashion. The mahogany card table was set with coffee service and cookies, and a deck of cards sat in the middle.

"Please sit here," Delphine said, indicating a chair that faced toward the front of the house. "I think you'll be most comfortable there. I'll sit across from you. Pauline, please take the seat at our guest's left. Laure should be here directly. May I offer you one of my cook's excellent wafers? I think you'll enjoy them."

Evangeline leaned forward to accept one of the delicate cookies from the proffered plate, thanking her hostess. She also accepted a cup of coffee.

She sipped at the coffee and nibbled at the cookie. Laure came into the room within seconds and took the coffee pot away.

"I'm sure this is going cold," she said. "Let me bring a new pot."

Evangeline's vision became blurry; it took her a while to ask what had been put in her cup. Then, just as Delphine had planned, Evangeline passed out. The bitter taste of the chicory coffee had masked the high dose of laudanum perfectly; Monsieur Dufilho, the apothecary, had blended the strong tincture for Doctor LaLaurie himself. The DuPre girl wouldn't wake up for hours. And if she didn't wake up at all? Well, that was the risk you took. Delphine had stood in Leonard's surgery for what felt like hours, trying to figure out the right medicine to render Evangeline unconscious. The ether had seemed to unpredictable, and the gases would have been dangerous to everyone else in the room. No, it had to be something that Evangeline, and Evangeline alone, would ingest. Delphine had enlisted her daughters in the deception of having her over for a card party.

"Hurry and help me get her out of this dress," she said to her daughters. "We'll have Bastien put her in the upstairs room with the nigras. No decent man will want to marry her once he finds out that she's spent the night in her underthings with a bunch of nigra men. She'll be ruined for good. After that, I'll approach Devereaux again about courting Pauline."

Laure unbuttoned the dimity dress while her sister held Evangeline up in the chair. Between the three of them, they managed to haul Evangeline out of her garments. They also removed her boots and stockings.

"I want to keep the dress, Maman," Laure said. "It's from Paris."

"If you want it, fine. If I had my way, she'd never need another dress again," Delphine replied. "Pauline's too thin for it; otherwise, I'd let her have it. We need to make sure she gets Alcide Devereaux's attention once his fiancée is ruined. Now, go find Bastien. He's strong enough to take the chit where I want her to be found. I'll put the boots and stockings out in the poor box."

Leonard LaLaurie, who had not gone to Plaquemines Parish at all, volunteered to take the items and dispose of them. He looked forward to whatever might happen next. Why, he might even go up to the slave attic later and make one of the blacks take the unconscious white girl while

LaLaurie watched. That would be an entertaining way to pass the wee hours of the night. It didn't matter in the least to him what Delphine or her daughters might think of that; they need never know. And, after all, the most important thing was that the DuPre girl was ruined; how she was ruined didn't matter in the least, either.

He drank his own dose of Dufilho's laudanum and went to bed, planning to get up later and visit the slave attic. Any number of things could happen up there ... and many already had.

Chapter Thirty-Four

April 10, 1834
Early Morning

Marie Arcante had watched Bastien, Delphine's light-skinned coachman, carry the white woman upstairs to what she thought of as the torture chamber over the cookhouse. The red-haired girl was wearing only her corded petticoat, stays, and sleeve plumper chemise; there was no telling where her dress, stockings, and shoes had gone. Marie couldn't move far, being literally chained to the stove. It was a reminder that her job was to cook: no more, no less.

"What you doin' with Miss Evangeline?" Everyone knew the DuPre girl, with her pretty red hair. She was reputed to be a kind woman who was good to her servants. The DuPre family had paid servants, and she'd heard that the two family slaves would be freed when Evangeline's father died; the crouch-backed cook wished she were one of them.

"Shut your mouth, *bossue*. This is none of your affair.*"*

The coachman had tossed the young woman's limp body into the room without care or concern and locked the door from the outside He left, laughing to himself as he hung the keys on a hook. Bastien hoped he'd be given a chance at the white girl when Madame and the doctor were through with her. White men were always going off with colored girls, after all; why shouldn't he do the same with one of their women? White whores in the Swamp didn't count, he told himself. This one was a Creole lady, and it would feel good to take her sort down a peg.

When he didn't come back after several hours, Marie decided there was only one thing she could do. She took a hot coal from the stove with a pair of heavy tongs and, reaching as far as she could, carefully dropped it on the pooled draperies that covered the slave quarters' window. She might die in the fire herself, but maybe the others would be saved.

Chapter Thirty-Six

April 10, 1834
10:00 AM

When Alcide arrived at the DuPre house for a planned visit with Evangeline, he was surprised to learn she was not at home.

"She went to the LaLauries' yesterday. I guess she decided to spend the night after supper, but that's really not something she'd do without sending a note," Monette informed him. "I think something must be wrong."

"Surely Evangeline would have sent word to me if she planned to cancel our outing," Alcide replied. "I'll stop by there on my way to the office; she may have fallen ill."

Alcide went back outside and took the reins of his black horse from the groom who held them. It was there that he was greeted by a young Black man.

"Been trying to catch up with you all night, sir," he said. "This is from my neighbor, Mademoiselle Marie Laveau." He spoke the *mo kouri mo vini* French dialect that so many New Orleans Blacks used. Invoking the voodoo queen was the surest way he could think of to make the tall

Creole man take him seriously. Ordinarily, one did not speak her name to the white folk.

"Thank you." Alcide gave the boy a picayune before he broke the seal on the note and read its brief contents. He swung up into the saddle and rode for Royal Street ... where he saw flames. He urged the little Arabian mare to a gallop and soon found himself opposite the LaLaurie house's slave quarters, which were on fire. Screams could be heard coming from inside.

When Evangeline awoke, she smelled smoke ... and something indescribable. She stood up despite leaden limbs and a headache, and looked around. She was in a room with seven Black slaves in various states of starvation and injury. The stench from feces and infected wounds was horrific. Worse, the men and women were shackled to the wall by collars and chains. Some of them looked as though they hadn't eaten in weeks.

"Mademoiselle DuPre," one of the young men gasped. "I don't mean to speak out of turn to a white lady, but what are we going to do?" Benjamin was only seventeen years old, and he was sure his life was over.

"I don't know, right off. However, I do know this: Delphine is mad, but Alcide will save us. Somehow."

Then, she started to scream for help as she banged her hands hard against the locked door. It didn't take long before her palms began to bleed, and yet she continued.

The slaves joined in, screaming and crying for help, as the room grew warmer and the smoke thickened.

Judge Canonge, Alcide's superior at the court house, was among the spectators on Hospital Street. When he saw Alcide, he came over to him right away and took the horse's reins.

"Devereaux, see if you can get in there and do something. I tried, but there was too much smoke. There are people in there; you can hear them screaming. That damn-fool LaLaurie told me it was none of my business when I asked him to help us, and his wife is taking jewels and furs out to her carriage without any slaves except that coachman of hers. It's very strange indeed."

Alcide would have hesitated, but then he heard a voice that he knew all too well: Evangeline was screaming from somewhere in that burning building. He slid from his horse, pulling off his coat, and raced inside. Another clerk from Canonge's office, Felix Lefebvre, was hot on his heels.

Men had already started a bucket brigade to subdue the fire, and a few of them followed Alcide and Felix inside. There, they found Marie, who told them that there were people locked upstairs and where the keys were. While Alcide opened the door, Felix freed Marie from the stove and helped her outside. Alcide carried Evangeline out to the street in his arms and sat her on the back of his horse before going inside to help the other seven people out.

Evangeline sat quietly on Alcide's mare, wiping her bloody hands on her petticoat. She'd burn it when she got home, she decided. Judge Canonge picked up Alcide's jacket from where he'd dropped it and handed it up to her so that she'd be covered. He continued holding the horse's reins until Alcide and the others had finished bringing the poor, miserable wretches out of the now-smoldering slave quarters.

Even though slavery was part of everyday life in the Quarter, the state of Delphine LaLaurie's slaves shocked her neighbors. She drove past them, Bastien whipping the coach horses into a frenzy, as they helped carry the starving men and women to the Cabildo yard so that they could get medical care. The coach was headed out of the Quarter and toward Bayou St. John; City Guardsmen on horseback tried and failed to catch them, and rode back quietly on their winded mounts.

Alcide, smelling of smoke, mounted his horse behind Evangeline and rode quietly back to the DuPre home with her in his arms.

"I was so scared, Alcide," Evangeline trembled in his arms. "I was frightened that you wouldn't come."

"I will always find you, Evangeline. Always. I swear it on my soul."

Chapter Thirty-Seven

Deep in the bayou country there are traditional healers called *traiteurs* or *traiteuses*. Theirs is a dying art, as the knowledge of herbal medicines disappears — along, in many cases, with the herbs themselves because of coastal erosion. These healers are also believed, in many cases, to possess second sight. — Diana Corbett, *Time Away*

Miss Julie opened her eyes. Diana was quiet and sleeping normally. What had felt like years passing was only a matter of an hour or two.

Amos still held Diana's hand on the other side of the bed.

"Come with me, baby. She'll be all right for a few minutes."

As they walked out of the room to the kitchen, shy cat Teddy hopped onto the bed and curled up next to Diana on the pillow. Miss Julie noticed.

"She must have something special; you know that cat doesn't make up to just anyone. Now, let me catch you up on what I saw."

It took Miss Julie about half an hour to explain all that had passed. "And you made her the most solemn promise anyone can make, Amos. You made that young woman your soulmate in the truest sense of the word, and it's stuck across the eternities."

If Amos was surprised by what his aunt told him, he didn't show it.

"That would explain why she seemed so familiar," he said. "We've been together before. Those dreams I had when I was little about saving a lady from a fire ... they were memories. And so many of us were there. Me, of course. You, John ... even Kelly. Somehow, I'm not surprised that she was Delphine LaLaurie."

"Indeed they were memories, Amos. Now, could you fetch me some of my headache remedy? I think Miss Diana and I are both going to need it."

Julie was already nursing a migraine; some of Diana's past life memories had flown by so fast that they were almost like a dream within a dream. Most likely, the scenes that lingered longest were the ones that were most important to her in her previous incarnation.

Amos went out to his aunt's workshop and stood there for awhile among the shelves. It was so much to take in. And yet, every bit of it rang true. It put so many things into perspective, including how he had been so sure that he had met Diana Corbett before that first day in the café. He couldn't help thinking they'd been brought together at this particular place and time for a reason.

Amos dabbed a bit of the headache remedy on Diana's temples. She was still sound asleep, but the thrashing and mumbling had stopped a long time before. Miss Julie was asleep on the front room sofa. Only Amos was wakeful. He paced the floor, stopping periodically to check on Diana again.

Miss Julie woke up after a while and came into the bedroom herself.

"Lord 'a' mercy, Amos. She's not a fairy tale princess waiting to be awakened by love's first kiss. You can leave her alone for a while. Get some rest."

"Tante Julie, I'm in love with her."

"I noticed," Julie replied drily. "And, in case you missed it, she feels the same way."

Amos paced the room, raking his fingers through his hair.

"But she's lived all over the world. She's been to places I've never seen. What would she want with some *couillon* swamp rat like me?"

"Don't make me put you over my knee like you're a child, Amos. Have you ever thought about what her life is really like?"

"Well, obviously I have, auntie."

"Hmm. All right. I reckon you know best."

Diana stirred a bit then. "Amos," she said weakly.

"I'm here, *chère*." He sat down on the bed. "What can I get you?"

"My medicine and things are at home, Amos." She sat up. "I need to go back to the apartment"

Miss Julie picked up the phone. "I'll call a taxi. You two are not taking that streetcar back to town."

When the cab arrived, Amos accompanied Diana back to Canal Street. He followed Diana into her bedroom and realized that, despite his many previous visits, he'd never actually been in there. At the foot of the bed was a folded nightgown, clearly a favorite; it was flannel, but had been washed so many times that the print was barely visible. The fabric was soft and light; it would be comfortable regardless of the weather. On top of it was a floppy, stuffed Dalmatian dog that had likewise been well-loved. He picked up the toy and put it aside so that he could help Diana into the nighty.

"That's my Pongo," Diana said as she took off her jeans and top. "I take him with me whenever I travel. It's hard to fall asleep in a new place sometimes, so having a comfort item helps. I've been telling my readers that for what seems like ages now."

Amos tugged the nightgown over Diana's head and helped her with the sleeves. She went into the bathroom to brush her teeth, and he sat down on the bed. He picked up Diana's stuffed dog and held it, thinking about what this so-called comfort item represented.

How could he not have realized how lonely Diana's life might be? Taking a plush toy with her all over the world for comfort was all the proof that he needed that his aunt had understood Diana perfectly. The part of him that imagined Diana's life to be one of constant glamour and excitement was silenced by the reality that she was very much alone in the world. In fact, now that he thought about it, none of the articles he'd read that first night showed Diana in any of the photographs. At no point did she seem to be part of the fun, or to have any friends enjoying the experiences with her. She shared everything with her readers, he realized, because she didn't have anyone else to share it with herself. It was quite a revelation.

He was also struck by one more recollection. In the article about her sojourn in San Francisco, Diana had taken a photograph from within a crowd. She was at a demonstration, seeking social justice for the homeless. Amos had glossed over it at the time, trying to take in as many articles as possible. He'd thought she'd done it to show a demonstration to her readers, but now he realized she was showing her readers that she had been demonstrating herself. Diana had used her position to try to further a cause she believed in by standing up and being counted, just as he did by feeding the hungry. Knowing now that she did this while facing an uphill battle with an exhausting disease filled his heart with admiration.

He also admitted to himself that Tante Julie had been right; he hadn't understood Diana's life at all. Now he had a glimpse inside, and could only approve of what he saw.

When Diana came back from the bathroom, she'd scrubbed the remaining makeup from her face and had her hair in a ponytail.

"I'll turn off the lights on my way out," Amos said as he rose.

"Please don't go, Amos. I would like you to stay here tonight. I don't feel ready to be by myself again."

"If that's what you want, I'll stay."

"Please."

Diana pulled back the quilt and slipped between the sheets while Amos stripped down to his briefs. He slid in beside Diana and turned off the bedside lamp before putting his arms around her. Diana fell asleep before he did, her head tucked under his chin.

Amos kept thinking about the things he'd considered earlier. Diana's life was so different from his own. Finally, he succumbed to the weariness that had teased at him for the past few hours and fell into a dreamless sleep.

Chapter Thirty-Eight

Sometimes it's fun to do something unexpected during a trip. Step out of your comfort zone. — Diana Corbett, *Time Away*

That Sunday morning, Amos got up early to make a light breakfast for Diana. He brought juice and toast to her bedside and woke her up.

"Thank you for staying with me," she said. "I must have sounded pretty foolish, not wanting to be alone."

"No, not really. I was glad to do it. I do need to go back home, though. I have some files to review for the Bayou Cultural Society, and need to get those into the office tomorrow. Will you be all right?"

"Yes, Amos, I will." It was on the tip of her tongue to say more, but she decided against it. Amos dressed, kissed her goodbye, and left her alone with her thoughts.

After she finished her breakfast, Diana got up to get dressed herself. Passing a mirror, she frowned.

"I don't want to be a redhead anymore," she announced to her reflection.

She booted up her computer and did a little research. Checking the clock, she realized she was in plenty of time. She made a call to a salon in the back of a Royal Street wig shop and they had time for her that day. It was time to make a change.

Amos did his best to keep his mind on the files in front of him. They were grant applications from Louisiana French immersion schools, and this was an important part of his work. He reviewed all applications that were being considered to make sure they were compliant with laws, Bayou Cultural Society policy, and so on. The truth was, they were dull as all get-out. He reminded himself that teaching the language to young people was the only way to keep it alive ... but that didn't change the fact that he was going out of his mind with boredom.

Maybe a walk would help; he could always come back to the St. Ann Street townhouse and finish his work later. He stepped outside and into the sunlight, with no particular destination in mind.

Before he knew it, he was standing inside a Royal Street antiques dealer he'd visited several times. On this occasion, money was tendered and a purchase made. When he went back to his apartment, Amos was far better able to focus on his work.

In fact, he was so focused that the doorbell ringing nearly made him jump out of his skin. He looked through the peephole to see Diana standing there. Her hair was a rich, chocolate brown and cut in a fashionable, long A-line bob that went just past her shoulders. He opened the door and took her in his arms.

"I'm glad you came by, *chère*. And don't you look as pretty as a basket of flowers! I love what you did with your hair."

"It's my real hair color," she said. "Your brother's going to have to give back that nickel when Jimmy finds out."

Amos laughed and closed the door behind the two of them.

"I'll just read while you work," Diana said, pulling a book out of her purse. "I don't want to interrupt. But I was so close by from where I had my hair done and, well, to be honest, I wanted to see you. If I'm in the way, you need to say so."

"You couldn't be more welcome," Amos replied. "Really and truly."

Diana was as good as her word; she read for a while and even nodded off. Amos noticed, and covered her with a quilt before going back to his files. When Amos woke her up after he'd finished his paperwork, she was a little embarrassed.

"I'm sorry," she said "I guess I was just that tired."

"No need to apologize, *chère*. Let me take you out to supper and get you back home after."

The two walked down to Jackson Square to a café where Amos claimed the cook made the best blackened flatiron steak anyone could ask for … but warned Diana that the Italian green beans were heavily laced with hot sauce, just in case. After dinner, they went back to Amos' home and made love until the wee hours of the morning. Nothing had ever felt more right to the two than being together, and now they understood why.

Chapter Thirty-Nine

Take advantage of opportunities to learn the history of whatever place you visit. — Diana Corbett, *Time Away*

Diana entered the Williams Research Center on Chartres Street that Monday and asked the receptionist for a reference librarian and a locker for her things. Before long, she was ensconced before a microfiche machine, going through newspapers and parish records from the 1830s and later. She was determined to learn everything she could about Evangeline DuPre and Alcide Devereaux.

She was soon taking notes fast and furious, using only the pencil and paper offered her by the librarian; there were strict rules about pens and such in the research center. She had so much to tell Amos.

Amos, in the mean while, was meeting with the president of the Bayou Cultural Society.

"I appreciate all the work you've done on these grants, Amos," Emilie Chenier told him. "It takes a load off of my mind to know how thorough you are. And I need your help with something else. The board has determined that the organization is going to need a dedicated public affairs professional to promote our work. We're looking at creating the position next year, and are budgeting accordingly. I was wondering whether you would consider the role. You'd be an ideal spokesman for us."

"I'm flattered, but I don't think I'm the person you want, Emilie. However, I may know someone who is. I'll get back to you."

He wasn't sure how he would present the idea to Diana, but he knew he had to try.

"Well, if you're sure. Your recommendation will go a long way with me, Amos. You know that," Emilie responded.

With only four days left on her visit, Diana stood with Amos in front of the Devereaux tomb in St. Louis Cemetery No. 2. They held hands as they read the names of Evangeline and Alcide, along with those of their children. The local cemetery guide had agreed to give them some time alone there, but would be back in fifteen minutes.

"Five, can you believe it?" Diana said quietly. "And the parish records say that only two of their children, a boy and a girl, lived. Evangeline died having the youngest one." She'd learned a great deal about the Devereaux and DuPre families in the course of her research. "Alcide never remarried. He and his two children became well-known abolitionists during the Civil War, which could not have left him popular in town. Still, he kept up his law practice and left it to his son. His daughter became president of the sugar cane plantation where she was born."

"Large families like mine were common in the old days; that's not so very many pregnancies when you think about it. Still, it's sad that he lost Evangeline to the last one. I guess she was the love of his life. He was a blessed man indeed."

Amos took a deep breath, which only served to remind him of what he'd put in his shirt pocket that morning. He'd been planning a far romantic setting for what he was about to say. Hell, even the zoo would have been better than a cemetery, he thought, but the time was at hand.

"I need to tell you something. I hate that you're leaving so soon. In fact, I hate that you're leaving at all, *chère*."

"I suppose we can use e-mail to keep in touch … and the phone of course." Diana felt awkward. Her imminent departure had always hung over their heads, but it didn't mean she enjoyed being reminded.

"Why couldn't you stay? I've been thinking about it, and it seems to me that that magazine work of yours could be done from anywhere."

"It probably could, yes … but I've got responsibilities in Seattle, too. I can't just drop everything." She couldn't decide whether or not she was flattered by Amos' words, and it showed on her face.

"I'm doing this all wrong, damn it. And this sure as hell isn't the place I wanted to do it, either. Miss Diana Corbett,

I'm asking you to make a life with me. I don't care where it is, as long as we're together. Seattle, New Orleans, or the dark side of the moon. I know it's soon to ask this of you, and I'll understand if you tell me I'm *couillon*-crazy. I love you, and I just can't stand the idea of not seeing you again."

He took the antique jewel box out of his pocket and opened it: inside was a gold ring, set with a ruby, surrounded by pearls. He'd bought it that day in the Royal Street antique shop when he knew it was the right ring at last. Taking a deep breath, Amos went down on one knee in front of her.

"Please, Diana … will you do me the very great honor of becoming my wife?"

"I … will," Diana said slowly, surprising herself a little. "And I love you right back, Amos Boudreaux. Now stand up and kiss me, you big *couillon*." Any other time, she would have called it infatuation and laughed it off, but Diana had never felt more sure of anything in her life.

He slid the ring onto her finger, then picked her up and spun her around.

"I'm the luckiest damn Cajun on this planet, *chère*." He sat her down, as he saw the guide was coming back and their time in the cemetery was coming to an end.

"Let me come with you to Seattle," he said. "I need to meet your people, after all … and then we can decide what to do next."

"We'll come back here, of course. That place of yours on St. Ann needs a woman's touch," she teased. "And you're right. My work can be done anywhere. Yours can't."

Chapter Forty

Seattle, Washington

Andrew and Rosemary Corbett waited in Sea-Tac's arrivals lounge with Diana's best childhood friend, Hope Rutherford. Diana had e-mailed them to give her flight information and ask if they'd meet her at the airport. It was in that e-mail that she told them about her new fiancé and said that he was coming home with her.

"I just can't imagine her getting engaged on such short notice," Hope opined. "It's simply not like her." She pushed a lock of blond hair behind her ear, not wanting to admit that she was a little jealous … and tired of being perpetually single.

"No, it's not," Rosemary agreed. "But she's certainly old enough to know her own mind. This Amos Boudreaux must be something really special."

Andrew harrumphed. "Doesn't make any sense to me either, Hope. Guess we'll all find out soon enough."

Hope craned her neck to look for her friend through the crowd, and eventually spotted her with one of the best-looking men Hope had ever seen. He was wearing a chalk stripe suit that fit so well it had to have been made for him, and was holding Diana's hand as though she was the most precious thing on the planet.

"Boy, do I hope there are more like that one at home," she whispered to Rosemary.

There wasn't time to say much more, because Diana let go of Amos' hand and rushed over to engulfed her friend in a hug. "I am so glad you came, Hopie. You have to promise to be in our wedding."

"You must be Amos," Andrew said, extending a hand. "Welcome to the family."

Chapter Forty-One

Christmas Eve
Spokane, Washington

"Diana, if you are going to mope around like that all evening I'm going to tell Santa Claus not to come," Rosemary said. "You're going to sap all of the Christmas spirit right out of this house."

"I'm sorry, Mom. I just got off the phone with Amos' sister, Annie. They're all out at his mom's place in Lafayette for Christmas and I'd hoped to talk to Amos. Annie said he wasn't able to make it out there because of bad weather. I got to talk with Jimmy, though. I had to thank him for my alligator. We didn't get to talk for too long, though. Harmon was getting ready to read 'The Night Before Christmas' to everyone."

Diana's Christmas package from Amos had included the ivory cashmere sweater she was wearing with a favorite pair of green slacks, and a stuffed alligator with a red ribbon around its neck. The toy had the biggest back paws she'd ever seen on a plush animal, and soft brown eyes A carefully penciled note, with a drawing that was clearly

Jimmy, Diana and Amos rendered in crayon, explained that Jimmy had picked out the toy at a shop near Amos' place on St. Ann Street so that Miss Diana wouldn't forget all about them while she was far away. Annie had added the ribbon so that Miss Diana would know he was a Christmas gator.

"They all sound like such dear people," Rosemary replied. "And it must be a huge disappointment not to be able to talk with Amos on Christmas Eve. Did you try ringing him at home?"

"Yes, and there was no answer. I know he's not at Miss Julie's; Annie told me that Miss Julie came out to Lafayette on the train ...and that Miss Pauline invited Antoine Robicheaux for Christmas breakfast. He was Miss Julie's sweetheart once and, well, maybe there's a little matchmaking going on there."

Diana smiled softly. "I'm being silly; he's probably over at the cathedral for services or something. I'm sure it's beautiful tonight." She twisted the ring on her left hand; she still wasn't quite used to wearing it, and found herself playing with it several times a day. Luckily, a jeweler had inspected it and made some minor repairs to the setting; it was as safe as any modern-day ring now.

"I'm sure you're right. Now, let's make some cookies or something, shall we?"

"Sure, Mom. Let me go get an apron." Diana headed for the pantry.

"Oh, darn. Andrew, I'm out of flour. Could you run to the store and get some?" Rosemary asked.

"Don't be silly, Mom. We don't need to make cookies. I know you're just doing this to keep me busy."

"I'll go," Andrew replied, grabbing his jacket from the coat tree near the door. "It won't take me more than a few minutes, and I'd sure like to have some cookies."

Diana went into the kitchen with her mother, where she knew the cookie jar was full to the brim.

"I just needed your dad out of the way so that you and I can talk," Rosemary said. "I worry about you, planning to go so far away. What's going to happen with that nice condo you have in Seattle?"

Diana outlined how Hope had agreed to buy the place, fully furnished, and that she'd promised her Toyota to a friend on the *Time Away* editorial staff who needed reliable transportation.

"Amos has this fancy sports car that he'd wanted since he was a kid, and we don't need more than one automobile. Plus, so many things are within walking distance of his home that it just seemed silly to me to keep it. As for going far away, you never worried about me when I was doing so much traveling."

"Oh yes, I did. Every single time you went away I worried. I worried about what would happen if you needed a doctor, or if you got hurt, or there was a disaster. It's what mothers do; we worry. And that doesn't stop just because your children grow up."

Diana reached out and hugged Rosemary.

"I love you, Mommy. The truth is, I am a little scared. I've always known I was coming home from those trips. It was what I held onto when I had to live someplace I hated, for the sake of the story. You and Daddy weren't really that far away, even after moving here. And Hope was in town for whenever I wanted company. Sometimes that condo of mine felt awfully empty, though. Being around Amos' family showed me how lonely my life has been."

"I love you right back, Diana Lillian Corbett. I'm proud of you and, the truth is, I'm a little jealous. I never did much traveling as a young woman. Then I met your daddy, and he's as much a homebody as I am. You've seen so much of the world. Now, you're going to live so far off. It's a good thing we have telephones and e-mail nowadays. A regular letter would just take so long to arrive that I'd be impatient.

"I admit, I'm a little concerned about you living in Louisiana. You know that if you and Amos try to start a family it won't be easy with your health situation, and there are some laws down there that, well … I just don't want to think any more about that. Amos is a good man, and I'm happy for you."

"What can be taking Daddy so long? The store isn't that far away," Diana observed.

"Well, maybe there are a lot of people there tonight, doing last minute shopping for Christmas dinner."

"I suppose that's so," Diana replied. "Still, you'd think he'd use the express line if he's just getting a sack of flour."

"Sending your father to the store for just one thing never works out; you know that he gets a dozen more items that he thinks we need every time. Why don't you go lie down in front of the fire? Honestly, you look exhausted. If you fall asleep, I promise to wake you when Daddy gets home."

Diana was tired; even though the flight from Seattle to Spokane was barely an hour long, she had to wrestle with her baggage and deal with the airport crowds. Still, she'd been enjoying talking with her parents and was reluctant to fall asleep. She knew that her father would cover her with a blanket and leave her on the couch rather than wake her.

"Let's listen to some Christmas albums," Rosemary suggested. She turned on the stereo, and put in some of Diana's childhood favorites. "I'll make some hot cider for the two of us."

Diana went back to the living room and sat watching the fire while she sipped her hot drink. Almost against her will, she started to doze off, so she put her mug on the side table and just let it happen. She was vaguely aware of the front door opening when her father came back, and footsteps next to the couch. Then, there was a whisper in her ear … a whisper with a musical accent that she would know anywhere.

"Well, well. If you aren't the prettiest Christmas present ever, *chère*. Just what I wanted."

Diana was immediately awake.

"Amos!" She wrapped her arms around him and kissed him enthusiastically.

"Merry Christmas, *chère*. I hope this is a good surprise." Amos shrugged out of his jacket, which was damp from snow falling outside. "I cooked this up with your mommy and daddy, and it looks to me like they kept the secret pretty well. My sister told Jimmy that Santa would never come again if he let the cat out of the bag, too. You know how that boy can chatter."

"You are the best present in the world, darling. Now and always. I love you, Amos Alcide Boudreaux."

Rosemary came out of the kitchen to offer Amos his own mug of cider. He was exhausted himself, having taken three planes to make his Christmas surprise for Diana happen. Before long, they all said their good nights and Amos followed Diana to the guest room with his luggage.

It was only after the door was closed and they were snuggled together in bed that Diana noticed the new tattoo around Amos' left ring finger: a tribal design with a stylized A and D in it.

"I was over on Frenchmen Street one day and decided to do it," he explained as he caressed Diana's cheek. "I didn't want to wait until I put the real ring on to feel married to you."

He was stopped from saying more by Diana's enthusiastic kisses.

Chapter Forty-Two

June

Vermilionville, Louisiana

"You surely do look nice in that lace dress, Miss Diana, I mean, Auntie Diana" Jimmy chattered. "Reckon my Uncle Amos is the luckiest guy in the world, marrying a pretty girl like you."

"I'm the luckiest girl in the world, Jimmy … because I'm getting you for a nephew." She bent down to hug him, and the photographer snapped yet another picture. "And you look handsome as can be in your tuxedo."

"Uncle Harm and me both have green ties to match the ladies' dresses," Jimmy said. "Mommy said that's the way you're supposed to do it. I saw Uncle Harm talkin' to your friend Miss Hope at the rehearsal dinner an awful lot. Do you think she'll be my auntie too? She's real nice. Course, Uncle Harm's older 'n her, but Mommy says you never can tell."

"Jimmy! You are going to wear Miss Diana out until she's too tired to become your auntie. Now, is everybody ready?" Annie was doing her last check. "You have all of the things you need, something old, something new, something borrowed, something blue?"

"I do." Diana couldn't help laughing at her response; she'd been practicing it all day.

"Well, then, *laissez les bon temps rouler!*" Annie smiled.

The organist began to play as Diana and her father came down the aisle of the Vermilionville chapel, following Annie, the matron of honor, and bridesmaid Hope. Both of the women wore floor-length gowns of emerald silk. Jimmy had gone ahead, solemnly carrying a pillow on which two gilt rings were sewn.

At the altar with the minister, and his brother Harmon as best man and Billy as groomsman, stood Amos in white tie and tails. At the first sight of Diana in her ivory lace sheath wedding dress, he found himself wiping away a joyful tear, and then repressing a smile … because metallic gold pumps peeped out from under the hem and his aunt's chandelier earrings sparkled under the veil.

During the reception at Vermilionville's Performance Center, Harmon stepped up to the microphone after everyone had eaten their supper to the tune of glasses being tapped so that Amos and Diana would kiss. Diana noticed Miss Julie talking to an older man with a long grey braid, and couldn't help wondering who he was.

"Now some of you may not know this," Harmon said, "but we're a pretty musical family."

There was a great deal of laughter at that.

"What the hell is that *couillon* up to?" Amos murmured in Diana's ear as he twisted the wide gold band on his finger. It would take some getting-used-to.

Jimmy came out to join Harmon, who held the mic down for the boy.

"Auntie Diana, Uncle Amos, we all practiced and practiced. Could everyone come and dance to '*Allons a Lafayette*,' please. Uncle Harm says it's a song about folks running off to get married. I'm gonna play triangle, and Grand-mama's gonna play Uncle Amos's squeezebox, and …"

"Reckon folks'll get the idea, son," Harmon interrupted as family members gathered instruments. "Baby brother, if you and that pretty bride of yours would lead off, please."

Diana's parents seemed a little overwhelmed, but they joined the other couples on the floor.

"I'm going to cut in on your daddy," Amos said, "so get ready to dance with him while I dance with your mama."

Seamlessly, Amos tapped his father-in-law on the shoulder and handed Diana over. Diana enjoyed dancing with her father for a little bit and the older man she'd noticed earlier cut in.

"I'm Antoine Robicheaux", he said. "Reckon I ought to introduce myself to the woman who's making dat *couillon* boy so happy," he teased. "For real-real, I'm happy for you bot', me."

"Mister Robicheaux ..."

"Tony, please, *chère*."

"I saw you talking with Miss Julie ... I understand there's some history there."

"Reckon we're a stiff-necked old pair. Still, she said she'd have supper with me later dis week."

The dance came to an end and everyone was seated, except for Jimmy, who ran over to Diana.

"Did you like our surprise, Auntie Diana? Did you?"

"It was just delightful." She hugged the boy, who ran back to his seat and beamed.

Harmon stepped back up to the mic. "The regular band will be on in just a minute. In the mean while, I'm going to tell some tales on young Amos, here ..."

When the dinner and dancing were done, Diana and Amos changed clothes for their "going-away," so that they could drive back to Hotel Monteleone on Royal Street to spend their wedding night before leaving the next day for a honeymoon in Paris.

Neither that night, nor on any other, did Diana dream of smoke and fire again.

Chapter Forty-Three

April
New Orleans

The native New Orleanians, or Yats, have a certain way of referring to people like me. They call us the "never-lefts." What they mean by that is that some part of our hearts stays in New Orleans until we come to live there for good. That's just what happened to me when I came here to do some of my "Temporary Local" features, and fell in love with the handsome Cajun to whom I am now married. — Diana Corbett Boudreaux, *Time Away*

Diana re-read the introduction of what would be her last article for *Time Away*. She'd accepted the full-time public affairs officer position with the Bayou Cultural Society, but had promised to do one more story.

It was the perfect start.

Emilie Chenier had told Diana that it was fine to continue writing for *Time Away*. However, Diana had good reasons for wanting to curtail her travel and so she'd decided to resign. Working in the office writing press releases and talking to the media was going to be an easy transition for someone who had lived all over the world and met all kinds of people in her travels.

Diana glanced at her watch and realized she needed to leave if she wanted to be on time for her appointment at her favorite salon, located in the back of the wig shop on Royal Street. It was a nice day for a walk.

The gossip and laughter at the salon always made Diana smile, and she loved the new look of her hair: pixie-short against the heat and humidity. She paid her fee and was saying her goodbyes when she felt faint. A look in the mirror showed her face beet-red despite the air conditioning. She pulled the phone out of her purse and handed it to her stylist, Johnny.

"Please call Amos," she gasped, and collapsed back into the chair.

It took both Amos and Johnny to get Diana into her husband's low-slung car so that he could take her to the hospital.

Amos had known Nick Gallier, the high-risk obstetrician, during his days at Tulane.

"I need to send her to her folks in Washington," he said. "If anything goes wrong with this pregnancy …" As he always did when he was stressed, Amos was raking his fingers through his thick, black hair.

"No, Amos. She can't travel. Not when her blood pressure has shot up like that this early. I don't want her lifting anything heavier than a loaf of bread, or taking exercise more strenuous than a walk around the block in the cool of the evening. In fact, I want her pretty much on bed rest as from today. I'll give her blood pressure meds and we'll watch her blood sugar just to be on the safe side.

"And if, God forbid, something goes wrong, I'll deal with the damn fools in Administration afterwards. Those idiots in the State House don't make it easy for people in your situation, that's for sure, with all their silly 'go home and think about it' laws. Women aren't stupid; they know what they want. I'm not going to lie to you, Amos; this is going to be hard on Diana."

"If anything happens to her, I'll go *couillon*-crazy," Amos replied.

"Then it's up to all of us to keep your wife and her pregnancy safe. You might want to consider not having any more after this one, though; her thyroid condition means she's always going to be high-risk. I'm going to keep her overnight just to be on the safe side; you can pick her up tomorrow."

Amos went back into Diana's hospital room to kiss her good-bye. "I'll be back tomorrow to get you, *chère*. They want to keep you for the night. Now, promise you'll rest." He dropped a kiss on her forehead, told her that he loved her, and walked out of the room.

In the parking garage, he stood for a long time looking at the Pantera and thinking about how hard it had been to get Diana in and out from it earlier … and how there was really no place to put a baby seat in it. He set his jaw as he got into his dream car and drove it for what he decided would be the last time. He took it to a dealer he knew in Metairie and traded it in on an elegant black Mercedes sedan.

Amos was a different man now from the brash young lawyer who wanted that show-off car, he realized. And that was all to the good.

When he got home, he pulled up a few more websites and made some calls. There was work to be done before Diana came home.

Nick insisted that Diana be brought out of the hospital in a wheelchair. Amos went to get the car while Diana waited on the sidewalk; she was shocked when he pulled up in the new sedan.

"Where is the Pantera," she asked as they pulled away from the hospital.

When Amos didn't say anything, she started to cry.

"You loved that car, Amos."

"Yes, I did. And at the end of the day it was just a thing. We need a car that you can get in and out of, and one where we can have a baby seat. A grown-up car, not a boy's toy."

Diana looked out the window of the new car as they drove home, trying to hide her tears from Amos. He was not fooled.

"*Chère*, are you really crying over a damn-fool automobile? I heard that pregnancy can make *couillon*-crazy emotions come up in a woman, but it was just a car."

"But it was your dream, Amos," she sniffled.

"No, honey. You're my dream. You and that baby of ours. Never lose sight of that." He reached across to put a hand on her knee. "And I just realized I haven't told you how nice you look with that new hairdo. Pretty as a picture."

"Don't you patronize me, Amos Boudreaux," she replied, but there was at least the beginning of a smile on her face.

"Hey, I'm told that most men don't notice their ladies' hairdos and would rather mess around with cars. I can't think of a better way to prove that false," he teased. "Besides, this way I won't be spending half my time with the car torn apart to work on it. Imagine that, *chère*. A husband who doesn't smell like motor oil every time his car acts up. That's got to be an improvement. Come on now."

Diana couldn't help but laugh at that.

"Well, that is something. Besides, it's kind of nice to be able to hear myself think; that Pantera was *loud*."

Amos helped her out of the car when they got home, and held the door open for her.

"There's one more surprise," he said as they went into the living room.

One of the leather chairs in the living room was gone. In its place was a beautiful chaise longue with a hardwood frame and dark brown damask upholstery. Its elegant lines were different from the masculine sofa and the other chair, but it still looked as though it belonged.

"I called a furniture store in Midtown and ordered it for rush delivery," Amos explained. "Nick Gallier says you need to be on bedrest, so I wanted you to have a place to put your feet up out here, too. I wanted to have everything set up just right."

Diana wrapped her arms around her husband's waist as he ruffled her hair.

"I love you, you big *couillon*," she whispered.

Chapter Forty-Four

New Orleans
May

Amos opened the door to let Jimmy and his mother into the apartment.

"Now, Jimmy, remember what you promised," Annie was saying.

"Yes'm. I'm not to plague Aunt Diana too much because she's having a hard time with this pregnancy and gets real tired."

Diana smiled from her beloved chaise longue. Her Hashimoto's disease had caused some early, potentially dangerous complications; as a result, she and Amos decided that this would be their only child, and he'd already made an appointment for himself to make sure of that. The ultrasound told them they were having a daughter; they decided to call her Evangeline.

"We'll be fine, Annie. I just wish I could join you for the Boogaloo. You know how I love the music." The annual Mid-City Bayou Boogaloo had become one of Diana's favorite things the first year she attended the free festival with Amos.

"I wish you could come too, *mon cœur*," Amos said before kissing her forehead. "But the doctor says no … and we can't leave Tante Julie and Uncle Antoine to run the Society booth on their own."

"I still can't get over them eloping right after y'all's wedding," Annie put in.

"It was about time," Amos laughed. "We'd better get out going. Are you sure you won't need anything? Annie's brought a muffuletta from Central Grocery for your lunch."

Diana promised she didn't, and kissed her husband goodbye.

"Reckon I can open a pop or pour a lemonade for Aunt Diana as good as anyone else," Jimmy asserted. "Plus, I've got books and things in my backpack so we can have a nice time. It won't be that long before Auntie Julie and Uncle Antoine are here to help anyway. And our sandwich is already cut in two; all I need to do is put it on plates."

Sitting on the floor next to Diana's chair, he opened the pack as Amos and Annie closed the door behind them.

"I've got a nice movie called 'The Princess and the Frog' for us to look at later. That's about New Orleans. There's some scary parts, but I'll warn you ahead of time in case you don't want to look. Oh, and I've got this book to read to my baby cousin 'Vangeline in there; 'Make Way for Ducklings,' that's a real good story. Uncle Amos said you lived in Boston for one of those articles you wrote, and it's about Boston and some ducks there."

Diana curled her hand around her belly and smiled contentedly as her nephew rambled on. It was going to be a perfect day.

Author's Note and Acknowledgements

I first became fascinated by New Orleans in 1973. That was the year Bobby Bare released "Marie Laveau," his novelty song about the voodoo queen. Throw in Jerry Reed's "Amos Moses" and Creedence Clearwater Revival's "Born on the Bayou," and I was hooked long before I heard a note of Zydeco or Cajun music or got past my fear of Cajun food thanks to a Baton Rouge-born colleague who showed me that it wasn't all about the cayenne pepper.

Still, I never imagined that I would fall so deeply in love with New Orleans as I did during my first visit, in 2016. I most assuredly left a piece of my heart there; a second research trip confirmed what will doubtless be a life-long love affair with the Crescent City.

The events of the LaLaurie mansion fire are true, although I have taken some liberties with the events leading up to it — and with adding a white woman to the list of those found by rescuers. The *Intelligencer* and other local newspapers listed a "Mr. D. —, a lawyer," as the man who led the rescue efforts for the slaves. I hope that avid historians will forgive me for displacing the real lawyer,

Amédée Ducatel, with Alcide Devereaux for purposes of this narrative.

While the Bayou Cultural Society is the product of my imagination, the movement to preserve Louisiana French and Louisiana Creole is not. You can visit the website for the Council for Development of French in Louisiana at www.codofil.org. In that vein, I also thank the Kouri-Vini and Cajun French discussion groups on Facebook for being so welcoming and sharing great information.

Likewise, what Amos tells Diana about the loss of coastal wetlands in Louisiana is very much true. If you would like more information, you can visit the Coastal Protection and Resource Authority website at coastal.la.gov.

Thanks to former colleagues Wanda Arceneaux and Carmen Gates for their insights about living in a place Carmen calls a "Bohemian banquet."

Thanks to legendary Cajun musician Doug Kershaw for being my Facebook friend. I am still starstruck whenever I think about it. That he subsequently entrusted me with one of his fiddles, a 1707 Guarnerius copy, is an indescribable honor. Doug, thanking you in person was one of the best days of my life. *Merci bien.*

I have many people in New Orleans to whom I likewise owe a debt of gratitude. So many, in fact, that the only way to do this is to make lists.

Musicians: Lee Benoit and the Benoit Family Band; Elliot "Stackman" Callier; Joe Lastie Family Gospel; Leroy

Jones and the Preservation Hall Jazz Masters; Sarah McCoy Trio; Radioactive Band; Rubin-Wilson Folk Explosion.

Guides and Historians: Alyssa Arnell; Joseph Donenfelser; James Hayes (and his lovely mule, Pearl); Ray Laskowitz; David Reichard; Wendell Stout, PhD; Capt. Brian Torres.

The staffs of: 1850s House; Backstreet Cultural Museum; Bamboula's; Bourbon French Parfumerie; Cabildo Museum; Chalmette Battlefield, Jean Lafitte National Park; Creole Queen; Historic New Orleans Collection; Historical Voodoo Museum; Hové Parfumerie, J.W. Marriott Hotel; Laura Plantation; Little Toy Shoppe (where I bought an irresistible plush alligator with enormous back paws); Louisiana Music Factory (especially Snooks, the shop cat); New Orleans Pharmacy Museum; Oak Alley Plantation; Place d'Armes Hotel (especially Stewart); Presbytère Museum; Spotted Cat Music Club; Royal Carriages; Tours by Isabelle; Voodoo Autentica, Williams Research Center.

Locally, I offer my thanks to the staff of Poor House Bistro, for keeping my memory stoked with outstanding Cajun food and the opportunity to hear more of Louisiana's music. Ditto to my friends Kathy Daniusis, Philip J. Tuley, and Deborah Hamouris, who recommended restaurants, night clubs, hotels, and so many more delights from their time living in NOLA themselves.

I not only relied on first-hand experience, but also the research available to me — both antique (W.E. Pedrick and Charles Gayarré's books, for example, were both published in 1885) and modern, popular and academic alike. Many thanks to the authors, film makers, and television producers whose work allowed me to give additional depth to my tale. A list of select resources from my research is in the next section.

The decision to give my heroine, Diana Corbett, an autoimmune disease was not undertaken lightly. Physicians estimate that 60 percent of women suffer from a thyroid disorder, and more than half of those are undiagnosed. Hashimoto's disease is the most common cause of hypothyroidism, and it can cause potentially fatal pregnancy complications. If I could make a plea to my readers, it would be to have their thyroids tested. My own Hashimoto's disease went undiagnosed for at least ten years.

As always, thanks to my husband, Jeff Cathcart, for his unwavering support. Thanks also to the Treehouse Adventure Writers, the best club I've ever joined. Finally, thanks to cover artist James Courtney and cover model Jason Aaron Baca for making this book a thing of beauty.

Selected Materials Used While Creating This Story

While writing this book, I relied on several secondary sources along with my primary source research. Here is a partial list. Many of these items were obtained from my local library.

<u>Books</u>

Ambrose, Herbert: *The French Quarter: An Informal History of the New Orleans Underworld*

Ambrose, Kala: *Spirits of New Orleans*

Brasseaux, Charles A.: *French, Cajun, Creole, Houma: A Primer of Francophone Louisiana*

Burst, Deborah: *Louisiana's Sacred Places*

Chase, John Churchill: *Frenchmen, Desire, Good Children ... and Other Streets of New Orleans!*

Clinton, Catherine: *The Plantation Mistress: Woman's World in the Old South*

Delaplaine, Andrew: *New Orleans 2016: The Delaplaine Long Weekend Guide*

Fodor's New Orleans 2016

Frommer's 2016 Easy Guide to New Orleans

Gayarré, Charles: *The Creoles of History and The Creoles of Romance: A Lecture Delivered in the Halls of Tulane University*

Gessler, Diana Hollingsworth: *Very New Orleans: A Celebration of History, Culture, and Cajun Country Charm*

Gill, James: *Lords of Misrule: Mardi Gras and the Politics of Race in New Orleans*

Gotham, Kevin Fox: *Authentic New Orleans: Tourism, Culture, and Race in the Big Easy*

Graham, Heather: *Why I Love New Orleans*

Harris, Joel Chandler: *Nights with Uncle Remus*

Hochschild, Arlie Russell: *Strangers in Their Own Land: Anger and Mourning on the American Right*

Krist, Gary: *Empire of Sin*

Lonely Planet's Pocket New Orleans

Long, Carolyn Morrow: *Madame LaLaurie: Mistress of the Haunted House*

Long, Carolyn Morrow: *A New Orleans Voudou Priestess: The Legend and Reality of Marie Laveau*

Longfellow, Henry Wadsworth: *Evangeline*

Love, Victoria Cosner, and Shannon, Lorelei: *Mad Madame LaLaurie: New Orleans' Most Famous Murderess Revealed*

Murphy, Michael, and Asher, Sally: *111 Places in New Orleans That You Must Not Miss*

Official New Orleans Visitors' Guide 2016

Oswell, Paul: *New Orleans Historic Hotels*

Pedrick, W.E.: *New Orleans as it Is*

Tallant, Robert: *Voodoo in New Orleans*
Taylor, Troy: *Haunted New Orleans*
Tidwell, Mike: *Bayou Farewell: The Rich Life and Tragic Death of Louisiana's Cajun Coast*
Voght, Lloyd: *A Young Person's Guide to New Orleans Houses*
Voisin, Gordon J.: *Cajun Vocabulation*

<u>Film Documentaries</u>
Plantation Portraits
Reconstructing Creole
This Ain't No Mouse Music

<u>Television Programs</u>
American Experience: New Orleans
American Patchwork: Cajun Country
Bizarre Foods America: New Orleans
Brothers Take New Orleans
Christmastime in New Orleans
Dancing to New Orleans
Delicious Destinations: NOLA
Tremé

Glossary

Au gratin - Baked and covered in cheese.

Beignet - A type of donut.

Bossue - Cripple.

Bourré - Card game, similar to Spades or Hearts.

Callas - Rice fritters.

Chèr/chère - Dear (masculine and feminine forms, respectively). Sometimes heard as *sha* or *shay*. Among the Cajuns, this is almost a reflexive expression.

Coffle - A group of slaves in shackles.

Couillon - Fool.

Crapaud - From the French word for frog, this game was named for way the dice jumped when thrown. Today, we call it craps.

Enceinte - Pregnant.

Etouffée - Smothered in spicy sauce.

Fais-do-do - A party with music and dancing. It comes from the French *fais dormi*, "go to sleep," signifying that this was an event that happened after children were abed.

Fyaer Mari - "Proud Mary" in Louisiana Creole.

Get down - Stop at one's destination. The term originated with stepping out of hansom cabs or, later, street cars.

Gumbo - Cajun or Creole stew. There are many types, with or without seafood or the okra from which the dish gets its name in the Wolof tongue.

Houma - A small Southern Louisiana Native American tribe.

Jazzy Pass - New Orleans bus and streetcar pass.

Jolie Blon - Pretty blonde.

Kaintock - A Creole slang term for Americans, specifically the rough trappers and riverboat men.

Krewe - A Mardi Gras parade club. The oldest ones are Mystic Krewe of Komus, and Rex.

Lagniappe - A little something extra.

Laissez les bon temps rouler - Let the good times roll!

Making groceries - Buying food. Again, this term originates in the French "*fais groceries*," which literally translates to "make groceries.."

Mo kouri mo vini - Literally "I go I come" in Louisiana Creole. This French patois is spoken by very few people nowadays and is considered an endangered language.

Mon cœur - My heart.

Mon 'tit cœur -My little heart.

Passe blanc/blanche - French. Literally, "passing as white."

Petit/petite - Small. When addressing a child, it takes on the meaning of "little one."

Plaçage - French for "placement." The term was used amongst Creoles to describe the custom of free women of color being placed as white men's mistresses. This was often a way around anti-miscegenation laws, in which a white person could not legally marry a person of color.

Plaçée - A free woman of color who was a white man's mistress.

Potager - Kitchen garden.

Roulaison - Cane-cutting season.

Rue - Street.

Sac-au-lait - French for "sack of milk." White crappie, a type of fish.

Saving dishes - Washing and putting the dishes away.

Tante - Aunt.

Tignon - Head scarf that all women of color were required by law to wear, whether free or slave.

Toot-toot - From the French "*tout en tout*," which means "all in all." It's the Cajun way of saying someone is your sweetheart, your everything.

Un cœur Acadien - An Acadian heart.

Veignt-et-un - French for Twenty-One. Nowadays also referred to as blackjack.

Where-y'at? -How are you?

Whistler's Walk - The path from the kitchen house to the main house. Slaves who carried food to the "big house" were required to whistle the entire time so that they could not taste the food.

About the Author

Books by award-winning, internationally published author Sharon E. Cathcart provide discerning readers of essays, fiction and non-fiction with a powerful, truthful literary experience.

Sharon lives in the Silicon Valley, California, with her husband and an assortment of rescue pets. She's been writing for as long as she can remember and always has at least one work in progress. Sharon is also a member of the Intergalactic Krewe of Chewbaccus, and the Music and Cultural Coalition of New Orleans.

To learn more about Sharon's work, please visit her blog at http://sharonecathcart.wordpress.com. You can also find her on Facebook, at http://www.facebook.com/sharon.e.cathcart.

Also by Sharon E. Cathcart

In The Eye of The Beholder: A Novel of the Phantom of the Opera
Through the Opera Glass*
The Eye of The Storm: A Novel of the Phantom of the Opera**
Seen Through the Phantom's Eyes
Les Pensées Dangereuses
Sui Generis
2010 Hindsight: A Year of Personal Growth, In Spite of Myself
Around the World in 80 Pages
Some Brief Advice for Indie Authors
The Rock Star in the Mirror (or, How David Bowie Ruined My Life)***
His Beloved Infidel
Brief Interludes
Clytie's Caller***
Hugs and Hisses: My Journey of Love as a Shelter Volunteer
Whispered Beginnings: A Clever Fiction Anthology (Contributor)
Live Life: A Daydreamer's Journal (Contributor)
Bestseller Bound Short Story Anthology, Vol. 1, Vol. 3 and Vol. 4 (Contributor)
Twelve Hours Later (Contributor)
Thirty Days Later (Contributor)
Born of War ... Dedicated to Peace (Co-author)

* Runner-Up, eFestival of Words Independent Book Awards
** Silver Medal, Global eBook Awards
*** Available in audiobook format

Made in the USA
San Bernardino, CA
02 September 2017